The Darkest Rose

A Leena Rose: Preternatural Investigator Novel

Brandon M. Thamke

United States

Leena Rose: Preternatural Investigator Novel

The Darkest Rose

This is a book of fiction. Names, characters, places, and incidents either are the product of the author's imagination or are used fictitiously, and any resemblance to actual persons, living or dead, business establishments, events, or locales is entirely coincidental.

The Darkest Rose

Cover artwork by: Rose Ink Press
Published by: Rose Ink Press – Brandon M. Thamke
Edited by: Rose Ink Press

ISBN: 978-1-7369565-6-4

A Vampire/Werewolf Hybrid, Homicide Detective is assigned to a case that unlocks a path of horror, hiding secrets from loved ones, and must deal with this all while maintaining sanity and trust.

Leena Rose has her hands full of murders, her first moon shift, lies, secrets and a vicious killer, never would she have thought it to be someone she once knew and loved, someone long thought to be dead...

The journey that I have with Leena and the team has been absolutely wonderful, eye opening. I'd go so far as to say it was life changing. With a few other ideas in the works as well as Leena's journey, I would love to give a shout out to family and friends for telling me that I have the talent, I have the creativeness and imagination. Thank you all for being the lit candle in any time of darkness.

Most of all, I would like to thank my husband. Thank you for telling me to keep going when I thought I wasn't getting anywhere, thank you for being my place of light when I need it. I look forward to continuing my journey with many more characters and stories as well as a wonderful team behind me.

1

The deep red color of the blood stained her protective suit, her face twisted at the grisly scene before her. The smell of brain matter turned her gut in ways she didn't think possible. An eye from the deceased, no longer in its socket looked deep into Leena's soul, at least that's how it felt for her. This poor victim sat in decay for well over three days before anyone found the body. An ill experienced eye would say a wild beast did this, a wolf possibly. Leena knew better, in ways that would soon affect her life and she didn't even know the events that were soon to unfold. She watched as the coroners took turns scooping the victim into bags, the splatting sound of body parts echoed in her ears as the occasional organ slid off their shovels.

Having just gotten off her toughest case to date, and with no time to herself, she was on to the next. She was, for a brief moment awarded a few minutes to catch up with Mark, her best friend, and the Medical Examiner. Hell, surrounding cities would call specifically asking for his help. Nothing escaped his view; he had a knack for spotting everything about a case, usually. Mark's eyes were an icy blue, like someone chiseled out small circles from a freshly frozen lake and placed them in his head. He loved them, his eyes that is, they forced everyone he came in contact with to know exactly what he is, a witch. He was a man of six feet, perfect sun colored blonde hair and though he hid them, he had abs that any man would kill for. Though they tried their hand at dating many years ago, the amicable split allowed them to remain the best of friends. The blaring of her phone broke their gabfest. Simultaneously rolling their eyes, she fumbled with her phone, clicking all the buttons she could. Leena had always hated smartphones; she hated the constant change companies did, and this form of technology was something she just couldn't wrap her head around. She hated how everyone was so addicted that they missed the world around them. She could never stand the fact that half the people in the world would never pick up a book anymore to read, they're all on some dumb app, just another excuse to have some form of electronic device in your hand.

"How many murders can happen in one damn day?" she barked through the phone at the innocent dispatcher.

Stepping to the side, behind a tree out of view, Leena pulled up a sleeve and ran a hand over her new wolf bite. Something she had been hiding for quite some time. Weeks ago, during a particularly intense full moon, Leena had a run in with her partner, James' fiancé, Matt. He had escaped his chains and though he had no knowledge of his actions, he was terrorizing a small park in eastern Coleman. Of course, Leena was called into action. Upon arrival, she was quick to recognize who this poor wolf was and made a feeble attempt to calm him. After a lengthy roll in the dirt, on a cold night, she successfully calmed him. James was called to help his fiancé and Leena walked off into the night. Was it wise to hide something that could change her, or even kill her? Of course not, but she knew this was something she had to deal with by herself, even though her friends would help within a heartbeat. If the new path were death, it would be a slow one anyway. So, why bother others with something uncontrollable?

"Hiding something?" Mark's voice snapped her back.

Wincing in pain, but hiding it from Mark, she pulled down the sleeve of her leather jacket and stepped into view. Her best friend always had a way of knowing when something was wrong. Magic aside, it was a separate gift he had.

"In these many lifetimes of knowing each other, have I ever treated you differently? Come on, spill!"

"You cannot, by any means tell James or Matt. Hell you can't even tell Captain Sommers! Got it!" Leena ripped him behind the same tree by his collar.

Pulling up her sleeve, again, she revealed the semi healed bite wound. Mark's mouth dropped, his eyes widened, and he took a small step back. His love and trust for his best friend left his body for just a moment. Hovering a hand over the wound, he could feel the supernatural energy emanating from her arm.

"How?" Mark pulled his hand back; fear filled his icy eyes.

"A few weeks ago, Matt attacked me."

Mark paused, ripped the phone from his pocket and in less time it took for her to stop him, he was on the phone with James. Boisterous shouting filled the area, Mark called James everything he possible could, even a few harsh supernatural names flew from his lips. After he was done with James, he took a turn on Matt. James, a usually calm Fey, or Faerie by nature, bit his tongue, holding back a few choice words of his own. He never cared for people who would attack his soon to be husband.

"I said no, Mark!" Leena ripped the phone from his hand, knocking him to the ground.

Crushing his new phone in the palm of her hand, she looked to her BFF and felt an urge she hadn't felt before. Her eyes shifted from gray to yellow with a small ring of emerald around the iris. Mark pulled himself away, across the cold ground, hoping she was smart enough to hold herself back. Slamming a fist into the tree, the striking pain snapped Leena back to reality.

"I'm sorry, Mark, really."

"This could kill you, fuck!" Mark's voice trembled. "Worse you could change."

"You don't think I know that!"

"Can you imagine life as a hybrid?" his voice coated with a hint of worry.

"It's something I have been thinking of. It scares the hell out of me, but there isn't anything I, nor anyone else can do. I have to accept my fate."

With the new case just across the street, both Leena and Mark walked as slowly as they could. Eyeing James in the distance, Mark couldn't help but imagine how nice it would it feel to crack his jaw. Leena knew what he was thinking and in her own special way, she convinced him to remain calm. James walked slowly up to his friend, with great caution. His eyes filled with sorrow; his posture was rather submissive. He didn't want to be hated, but even more so he didn't want the love of his life to be shunned. Even in this manner, James was still one of the most handsome beings that most people have seen. As like any faerie, he was perfection. His hair was always done perfectly, his posture almost always model like and his body, now that was a body to desire. Perfectly chiseled abs and pectorals had many assuming that he chose the wrong profession. Recruited many years ago by a modeling agency, he turned it down to follow his late father's footsteps. Old man Shayla, James' father was taken from him by what many call The Sickness. A horrid disease that rots vampires from the inside out. A cause of the lack of blood or worse yet, a disease created by the Anti-Vampire Association, but in creatures such as a faerie, it ultimately kills them slowly. Causing one to live in a state of fear and deliria, he was locked away in a room, fed through a slit in the door and hardly seen by anyone. It almost killed James to see his father in such a way.

They've lived years without the AVA as James made it a point to hunt them down. In the end it was discovered that they had either disbanded or in many opinions, they were hunted by vampires and nightwalkers, a breed of vampire that suffer from The Sickness, yet haven't fully succumbed to the awful results of the disease.

Nightwalkers were unfathomably strong, their thirst for blood, whether it was to feed or just kill was out of this world. A few more steps and Leena was frozen in place, a fragrance she hadn't caught in a while filled her nasal passages. She looked around the park, her nose pointed to the sky. She truly looked like a hunting dog. Finding the scent, she followed it as Mark and James made way to the scene.

"Sam? Samuel?" she questioned; her brow furrowed.

"Hey, love," his large smile both filled her heart with warmth and anger.

She walked as calmly as she could in his direction. Extending arms for a warm embrace, Samuel wasn't expecting the next series of events. Thrusting a palm into his chest, Samuel stumbled to the ground, his eyes wide, shock stretched across his face. Lifting him by his shirt, his feet were left kicking in search of the ground. Allowing an unnecessary amount of anger to consume her, she felt a few bones break as her fist connected hard with Samuel's jaw. Falling like a rag doll to the ground, she gave a swift kick to his side, forcing him to his feet. She wasn't finished, but he was saved by another, someone else she hadn't seen in some time.

She eyed the man, tall, muscular, and black shoulder length hair. A vampire, her creator to be exact. Raphael was old, older than anyone could figure out and he made it a point to never give that away. During a war, long ago between two lands, Leena was caught between crossfire and injured beyond what anyone could take care of. Feeling pity and a hint of love, Raphael turned her and took her under his wing. They spent hundreds and hundreds of years together, feeding, screwing, and ruling all they could. He was best known as the King of Coleman.

"What the hell?" she barked. "Long time, no see… that goes for you both!"

"As I said in my letters, which you clearly didn't get, I couldn't tell you why I left," Samuel did his best to explain.

"As for me, well, I'm a busy guy," Raphael left it at that and yet Leena still felt a pull of lust, for both of them.

Leena knew she was a sexual woman, something she couldn't control, or didn't want to. She could have many lovers, men, and women, in fact she took pride in being as open as she is. However, seeing two of her past lovers in one place was a slight shock.

"Samuel, why are you here?"

"The victim had an address in Claresville and being Chief Blackhorn, I was called once they identified the body. There is still a great deal of work to be done."

"Let me guess, after this you leave again?"

He placed a hand to Leena's shoulder. "I can't tell you, but now that you are here my work is done."

Leena once again watched as he walked off and the familiar scents soon faded away. The sounds of rushing footsteps grabbed her attention, causing her to spin on her heels. Mark and James were rushing in her direction, looks of disgust rested on their faces.

"This one is intense… wait who were you talking to?" Mark slowed down.

"Samuel and Raphael."

"What?" James raised a brow. "Samuel peaced out a while ago and Raphael is far too busy to attend something like this. Not to mention he is an ass."

Leena shook thoughts from her mind. "What are we dealing with?"

The three walked to the crime scene, ducked under the caution tape, and eyed one of the more gruesome views they had ever seen.

"So, what have we got?" she asked harshly. She knelt by the body bag, pulled back the top and with a swift action she covered her mouth. The scene and smell caused her to gag. Fighting back her lunch, she stood and did her best to catch her breath. A man covered in lacerations, bites, and blood rested just under the bag. Missing an eye and a large part of his jaw had Leena wondering how the hell someone had the ability to recognize this man. His teeth were removed and to everyone's dismay, he was missing most of the lower half of his body. His fingerprints were burned, and hands broken. Gathering another round of courage, she examined the body as Mark went to grab some supplies. A note, to perfect to be with the body sat just inside the man's breast pocket. Sneaking the note from the dead man, she took a few steps away and opened the letter.

"Leena, I must say that this kill will remain one of my favorites. I know your secret. I think I will continue to have some fun. Soon the truth will come out. Whether I kill more is entirely up to you. – The Darkest Rose," Leena read to herself, mouthing the horrifying words. "Fuck," she whispered harshly.

"What?"

Mark's question startled Leena. Pointing to the note, he pushed her for words. Handing the paper to Mark, she remained silent, allowing the fear to fill his soul.

"The Darkest Rose?" he asked.

"I don't know," she lied.

Leena knew all too well who this was, and she knew that saying anything directly would put a lot at risk, including many lives. It's bad enough there were already many in danger and she had no way to help all of them. She knew she needed to keep the true identity of The Darkest Rose at bay.

Long hours passed and night began to fall, the cicadas stopped buzzing, which was odd to many as it should've been far too cold for cicadas to be around. The crickets started to sing, and the night air grew stale. Those who could began to pack up their equipment as onlooking bystanders went to their homes. Knowing her weekend was to be a bore, she called a cab. Leena hated calling a taxi, they always looked to the side never accepting a vampire as a passenger for fear of being compelled. Hearing the popping of the exhaust, she watched the cab pull up to the curb.

"Good evening."

"Evening sir, I need a ride to Third Street, south of Main."

"I can't help, sorry," the cabbie spit out his words in less than a heartbeat.

"I'm sorry?" she asked.

The driver pointed to a sign just above the dashboard reading "NVA" short for "No Vampires Allowed". It's easy to spot when someone is a vampire, the dead giveaway is the abnormally pale skin tone, gray eyes and ever showing fangs that grow longer when hungry or angry.

"Sir it has been a very long day."

"Rules are rules," he yelped speeding off into the night. She felt herself growing tiresome and angry, which for her is not usually a good combination. She sighed, stepped off the curb and in the same motion leapt back to safety. James came speeding around the corner, missing car after car, forcing a few pedestrians to scream.

"Watch where you are going, dumbass!" screamed a woman waving her hands in the air as a man threw his soda at the rear window. He couldn't have cared less; he was on a mission.

"Leena, get in!"

"Why?"

"We're escaping for the weekend," Mark spoke from the back seat.

Taking the opportunity to get the day off of her brain, she slid into the vehicle. Mark looked to his friend as Matt and James laughed and sang loudly in the front seats. Ignoring Mark, she could feel him trying to wiggle his way into her thoughts. Years of practice had allowed Leena to build psychic walls to prevent anyone from gathering her thoughts or knowing how she truly felt about things. Mark, however, was far more experienced and had his ways. It didn't always work, but she was exhausted and couldn't fight back.

"I know who that is. It took me a while, but I figured it out," Mark's voice rang in her head.

"Don't say anything to anyone, got it," she whispered back.

Interrupting, James asked how they were doing, and Matt pulled out a pamphlet for their current destination. Pointing out the address, he made sure that James knew precisely where he needed to be going. Continuing their love filled laughter and riotous singing, Leena looked out the window.

Relaxing herself, she inhaled deeply. "So, what is this Fall Festival?"

"Something Midland does every year. The buildings, houses and streets are all decked out in the greatest fall décor. People from all over come to Midland to see the sheer beauty of the place."

"And we are staying downtown. We have rooms for all of us. We all need to get away," Matt smiled in the pull-down mirror.

2

The relaxing, long weekend came to an end. Leena, Mark, Matt, and James all laughed, filling the vehicle with happiness. Something they desperately needed. Pulling into the apartment parking lot, James threw the Jeep in park. Turning down the music he looked around at his friends, smiling. Stepping out of the vehicle they all stood under the awning, rubbing their hands together for warmth.

"I had fun this weekend, thank you," Leena expressed.

"Next week is the Coleman Fall Festival and you can bet your bottom dollar that we will all be going," Mark smiled at Leena. "Oh, and if you can find him, bring Raphael or Samuel, or both."

"Sounds perfect," James and Matt added. Hugging their friends, they climbed back into the vehicle, making their way home. Waving goodbye as they pulled away both Leena and Mark crossed the street entering a nearby park.

Crossing the small bridge over to the path, they sat on a bench looking at the moon, the snow-covered hills and listened to the traffic making its way through town. Snapping his fingers, a thermos of hot chocolate and a flask of Dr. Plasma manifested themselves just beside Mark's lap. Handing the drink to Leena, he smiled as he knew doing magic in public was risky.

"Thanks, so why are you okay with Raphael or even Samuel coming to the festival next week?" she asked as she sipped on the Dr. Plasma, a synthetic form of blood.

"After the past few days seeing how happy James is with Matt, it made me think that everyone deserves something like that. Maybe I will find it one day," he spoke softly.

"I'm no romantic, but Mark I am sure you will. You were one hell of a romantic when we were together," she added.

"Well let's hope, I actually got a card from Bella Fawn when we were at that Fall Festival. I am thinking of giving her a call and, well I will just wing it from there."

"Fawn as in Luna the shop owner?"

"Yeah, Bella is her daughter. She is actually a witch!"

"They all say that," she laughed.

"No, really. She was doing a reading for me and of course I laughed. I asked her what card I had got, and she told me Seven of Swords."

"Okay?"

"She explained what it had meant. Naturally, I am aware of what the tarot cards mean. After I allowed her to read the cards, we had a small conversation where I found out who she was. Getting ready to leave she grabbed my arm and was forced into a vision, a premonition if you will."

"So, what happened?" Leena turned on the bench getting readjusted.

"She said she saw a man in an apartment or a small room as flashes of the Seven of Swords surrounded the man. She couldn't catch a name and as it was blurry, she couldn't make out what the man looked like," Mark added as he looked up at the sky.

Walking around the park they saw fish in the pond that hadn't quite frozen over and a film of frost covering the petals of the various flowers that weren't ready to leave for the winter. They walked for a good two hours talking about the future and even bringing up a few things from the past. The cold began to grow too much for them, leaving Mark to call for a cab. Standing in the snow, which started the night before and hadn't stopped since, they patiently awaited the arrival of the taxi.

###

"Good evening, sir," the plump driver spoke as a cough left his mouth, slamming the car into park as he approached the curb.

"Evening," Mark added. Looking to Leena, he gave her a hug as he climbed into the car.

"Have a good night," she waved.

Telling the driver where he lived, Mark stuck his hand out the window waving goodbye to Leena. Taking a deep breath, she made her way back to the bridge. Looking over the edge she saw a shadow in her reflection. Spinning around, she slipped on the bridge, but was caught by a pair of muscled hands.

"Where the hell did you come from?" she laughed.

"Felt like I needed to talk to you. So, I walked to your apartment and saw you talking with Mark."

"You waited patiently for me?" she asked, eyebrow slightly raised.

"Of course. I wanted to see you. Leena I," his conversation was brought to an abrupt stop as she put her hand in the air.

"Raphael, no! Not now, why are you being so gushy?" she steadied herself, fixing her shirt.

"I get it," his voice lowered as he looked away.

Placing a hand on his shoulder, she lightly kissed his cheek. Feeling the warmth of her lips he cracked a smile. Once again sitting on a bench he looked at Leena as she was taking in the night life. Coleman may have had its crime, but an average night was calm, beautiful, and even joyous at times. She loved where she lived.

"What's going through your mind?" he asked.

"As much as I love my apartment, I want to get out."

"So, move in with me," he spoke softly.

Looking at him as if he had insulted her, she chuckled lightly. Standing up to stretch she walked away, leaned against a tree, and looked at Raphael. Still assuming he was crazy, she put a hand up as he tried to confront her.

"We aren't a thing Raphe."

"As you keep bringing that to my attention, I am painfully aware. I don't want you to move in with me that way, I want you to move in with me, so you have more space. It would still be your own place; you can do whatever you want with it. I am hardly there; I have other things I tend to. Kingship can keep a vampire pretty busy," he laughed.

"Maybe, let me think about it. I work a great deal and having a bar below me could get irritating," she added.

"Right, but I own that, it won't be anything like the previous owner. Free drinks, free food and free entry," he spoke trying to outweigh the cons.

"Fine, but I have certain demands. For starters we change the place up a bit, not much, but just enough!"

"Deal," he smiled.

"And two, there are no mass feedings to ever take place. If I see one thing out of the ordinary, I will take the place down. That's a promise," she spoke demandingly.

Agreeing to all her demands he was left smiling as he pulled her in for a muscle filled hug. Letting her arms dangle by her side she grew tired and pulled away. Giving a final goodbye for the night, she brushed the hair from his eyes and made her way to the front door of her apartment. Turning around to give a last-minute wave she saw that he had disappeared into the shadows. Laughing to herself quietly she shook her head as she ascended the stairs. Before she had a chance to enter her place she was stopped by her elder neighbor.

"Good evening, Mrs. Johnson."

"Good evening sweet child," her lips pursed into a tight smile.

"How have you been?"

"Same old, same old. I deal with arthritis on a daily sweetie. Where have you been off to these past few days? Has a young man been courting you?" she continued to smile.

"No ma'am, I have been with some friends is all. Went to the slopes a few days ago and spent the day at the Plaza Mall. It's been a relaxing few days," Leena lied softly.

"That's good young lady, after what happened here the other night I was wondering when you would be taking some time for yourself."

"Speaking of that, I guess I owe you an apology. I owe the building an apology really. I don't think any of us were expecting to be attacked by a rouge pack of Nightwalkers."

"Leena, I have been around for many years. In fact, I voted for the equality of supernatural beings. With as deaf as I am becoming, your little fight was nothing in my mind," Mrs. Johnson laughed.

Spending a few moments to talk a bit more with Mrs. Johnson, she was soon offered tea. Turning it down, Leena was soon sucked into hearing about the good old days, her late husband and how awesome she was in the fifties. Stories of her dancing and flower power days filled Leena's ears as she stood patiently waiting for Mrs. Johnson to finish. As Mrs. Johnson paused for a moment Leena saw an opportunity to sneak in.

"Mrs. Johnson?" she asked.

"Yes dear?"

"I have to be up early. Meeting friends again for breakfast and then ice-skating," Leena quickly lied, again.

Giving her a hug goodnight, Leena quickly hugged her back. She may be a badass soon to be hybrid, at least she hoped that was what would happen and not death, but she had a special place in her heart for Mrs. Johnson. Turning towards her door, she inhaled deeply, letting out a sigh of exhaustion.

3

As Leena stood in front of her apartment she fumbled for the keys, unlocked the door, and fell into her living room. Brushing the hair from her eyes she locked the handle and slid the chain across the door for extra security. Making her way to the kitchen she was brought to a halt as a familiar scent caught her attention. She hadn't recognized this scent in a thousand years. Making her hair stand on end she turned towards the chair in the corner by her bookshelf as yellow-orange eyes looked up meeting her gaze. Recognizing who it was, fear, worry and many other emotions filled her head. Leena attempted to move, but was frozen in place, her breathing was now uneasy and heavy, like one gets before stepping foot in a haunted house.

"Philip?" Leena spoke, fear rushed over her as a crooked smile grew on the man's face, an evil presence filled the room.

"Hi," his eyes grew dark.

Leena stood with her back against the door, fear, anger, and sadness began to consume her. She shook her head hoping that when she opened her eyes her murderous brother would vanish. Her eyes opened, and a sigh of dread escaped her lungs, Philip, to her dismay was now standing in the corner. She had no time to blink before Philip was within arm's reach of her. Attempting to become one with the door, she did everything she could to back out of the way and avoid his grasp. Swiftly moving to where Philip was once standing, she grabbed her gun, pointed in his direction, and allowed anger to consume her soul. Fangs growing, she began to almost hiss as she was prepared to defend herself.

"I've killed a lot of people, Leena," he sneered happily. "All to get your attention, you've become quite dull for being over one thousand years old, sister," Philip's eyes seemed to darken.

Leena was left speechless; all she could do was stand her ground. Looking over to her shelf she saw her letter opener, remembering that she had used it during the attack of the Nightwalkers, she quickly reached for the weapon and as swiftly as she could, threw it at Philip. Unable to react, he was filled with a piercing pain. Ripping the blade from his shoulder, he tossed it up in the air, juggling it for a moment. Catching the opener by the tip of the blade, he hurled it in her direction. Quickly leaping at Leena, he grabbed the blade from the air, landing hard in front of his sister.

Plunging the letter opener into Leena's stomach, he left the blade as he grabbed her neck, tossing her back across the living room. Writhing in pain on the floor as a pool of blood formed under her, she looked up to Philip who was slowly but eerily walking over to her. Kneeling to meet her gaze, he placed his hand on the blade, twisting, slowly. Leena screamed, placing her hand near her wound, she used the other hand to thrust her palm into Philip's nose. Feeling the bone break under her hand, she used what strength she could, kicking Philip over the couch.

As the apartment complex was new, only a couple years old, it was unfortunate for Leena as they constructed the building with abnormally thick walls, she knew that the chances of anyone hearing her screams were slim to none, more so since most had left for various fall events. Using the arm of the couch to help himself off the floor, he pushed it aside, again making eye contact with his sister. Kicking her gun to the side, he slowly picked her up off the floor, grabbed the blade, pulled it from her body and with no hesitation he plunged it once more just inches away from her heart.

"Why?" she cringed as a singular tear fell down her cheek.

"Why? Why!" he barked, turning the blade allowing it to slightly nick the heart.

Losing breath, she attempted to kick herself away. Enjoying the torment he was inflicting upon Leena, he smiled, allowing fangs much like hers to bare themselves and glisten in the light. Gaining a chance to brace herself, she grabbed his wrist, twisted his arm away from her throat, placed her feet against his chest and pushed as hard as she could. Falling hard on the floor, she stumbled, bumping into the coffee table which pushed the blade in further. Philip was quickly gaining his balance, glaring at Leena.

"You left me! Me, your own flesh, and blood! You couldn't even bring me with you! Couldn't even give me a proper burial!" anger filled his voice as he was once again pushing her against a wall, using his forearm against her neck to hold her in place.

"You were dead, Philip! I had no choice; Raphael and I had no choice!" she choked.

Disregarding her plea, he tore the blade from her body once again nicking her heart, leaving blood to pour from the wound. As she hadn't fed in a while, her wounds were not healing as fast as she had expected. Falling to her knees, she tried for her gun but found herself once again filled with pain as Philip crushed her hand under his boot. Using her free hand, she tried to lift his leg, but found herself being dragged to the kitchen by her hair. Throwing her against the cupboard, he tipped her head back, grabbed an herb mixture from his pocket and mixed it with some water. Leena tried to escape but failed as Philip began to pour the monkshood and hawthorn concoction down her throat. Feeling the burning sensation, she slowly crawled away, spitting up the poisonous herbs.

"This is just a taste of the pain that I will be bringing to you. I'm back, selfish bitch and there isn't anything you can do. I will spend eternity torturing you, blackmailing you and leaving you to wish that you were dead. I will go after everyone you care about, leaving bodies in every direction," Philip, knife firmly grasped in hand, thrust his arm in the air.

Immediately bringing the blade back down to inflict pain once more on his sister, he was brought to a halt. He used his other hand to try and push the blade into her back, but he couldn't as paralysis was quickly taking control of his body. Mark stepped from the shadows of the hallway, arms crossing his chest he magically and without Philip's knowledge claimed control of his body. Looking up, fear filled his eyes as he witnessed Mark standing just inside the apartment. Now, with an extended hand he muttered an unrecognizable word, closed his fist which seemed to now leave Philip writhing in pain on the floor. Dragging herself away from her brother, she watched as Mark took a few steps closer, repeatedly muttering the same word. It looked as if, with every word that was spoken, each bone in Philip's body was being snapped in half.

Screaming in pain, he looked up to Mark, blood trickling from his ears. Mark was attempting to use magic to dry Philip out. Eyes changing to the eerie yellow orange, he lunged in Mark's direction. Driving his fangs deep into Mark's neck, he found himself flying back into the kitchen, breaking the cupboard, and chipping the porcelain sink. Forcing Philip to arch his back in pain, he dug his hands into the floorboards, jumped at Mark who once again quickly raised his hand, seeming to freeze Philip mid jump. Without skipping a beat, Mark tossed his hand to the side and as a result, threw Philip out of the window, glass exploding in every direction.

Rushing to the window, he leaned over, being careful enough to not cut his hands, he looked for any sign of Philip. Glass was scattered across the ground, but there was no evidence of the murderous maniac anywhere. Realizing his best friend was still on the floor, he rushed over to her, kneeling beside her, he slowly placed her head on his thighs. Noticing her wounds were still pouring blood, he grabbed a small piece of glass, cut his palm, and lightly placed his hand over her mouth, allowing her to feed. Her wounds slowly began to heal, her breath was beginning to steady.

"Thank you," she looked up, gently pulling his hand away.

"What the hell happened? I was at my place when I had realized I forgot one of my grimoires here a while back," he spoke, helping Leena up off the floor, walking her to the couch.

"I'm not sure. You left and not long after Raphael showed up. We talked, he did some flirting, nothing unusual. He asked me to move in with him, even changed the name of the bar to Eternal Night."

"Hmm, fits perfectly," Mark laughed, rolling his eyes.

"Sure, we'll go with that. Don't you find it odd that the moment I think of letting him close, I am attacked by my "dead" brother? The same brother that I was told didn't make it because he was already taken by Death," Leena fixed her hair, wounds still taking their time to heal.

"Do you think we should postpone future events like the Coleman Fall Festival?" he asked slowly.

"No! The last thing we need is to bring something like this back to the precinct. We will take care of Philip; we need to keep this as far away from Captain Sommers as possible."

"What exactly did your brother say to you?"

"He isn't my brother! Not anymore!" Leena barked.

"Sorry," his hands went up in a way of surrender.

"He blatantly stated that he will spend the rest of our lives torturing me, blackmailing in any way possible and leaving me to wish that I had died all those years ago. He wants to go after everyone I care about!"

"Well, thankfully you don't care about a great deal of people. If any at all."

"I care about you, if I didn't, you wouldn't be my best friend," Leena explained softly. She looked defeated.

"Leena, I know that. You don't need to worry about me, as shown I can protect myself against Philip."

"You got lucky tonight, now he is pissed. He had horrible tantrums when he was younger, I don't really want to picture what a one thousand plus year old hybrid will act like when he doesn't get his way," she allowed an exceedingly small chuckle to escape her lips.

They spent the rest of the night waiting for Leena's wounds to heal. Considering herself to be lucky, she slowly and cautiously walked to the fridge, grabbed herself a Dr. Plasma and a can of soda for Mark. It was a cold night, a silent night. With fear in their minds they didn't move around much, just enough to grab blankets and discuss whether she should move in with Raphael. If not for convenience, then possibly for extra protection.

4

The next morning brought a chill in the air, accompanied by the second heavy snowfall of the year. Lack of glass in her window allowed for the air to creep into the apartment, awakening them from a deep slumber. Shivering under their king size comforters, they stretched, trying their hardest to keep the heat under the blankets. Mark rolled over, ignoring the cold, ignoring the alarm, he begged for more sleep. Leena smiled, happily shaking her head at Mark, who in that moment resembled a child refusing to wake up during school break. Allowing him to sleep, she made her way to the bathroom.

Twisting the nozzle on the faucet, she ran her hand under the water, letting it change from cold to hot, she found the perfect temperature. As the water ran down her shoulders, she could only think of last night's attack, her slow healing wounds, and Raphael's request. Flashes flew through her mind but were soon interrupted by the blaring music from her phone. Jumping from the shower she slid across the bathroom, plowed through the door, and stopped at the kitchen table.

"Hey," she answered, catching her breath.

"You alright?"

"What? Oh, yeah I'm okay," she pulled her wet hair to the side.

Continuing her conversation with James, she happily left out the run in with Philip the prior night. Looking back into the living room, she saw what could only be explained as a tornado making its way through the middle of her apartment, it was disastrous, an unbelievable mess. Leena listened to James talk as she allowed herself to think of all the positive ways that moving could benefit her. Watching Mark stretch and hide his head under the blanket, she snuck into her room, dropped her towel, looked in the mirror and checked out a few of her scars. Scars left long before she was turned. Rubbing her fingers along them, Leena shook her head as she tossed on her undergarments, threw on a white t-shirt and cargo pants. Remembering her combat boots were next to the door, she made her way to the couch, gently stepping over her best friend.

"Leena?" Mark was slowly waking up, rubbing the sleep from his eyes.

"Right here."

"I think we need to go get some coffee!" he spoke, tilting his head to the side allowing it to snap and pop.

"Order from the café?" she begged.

"Or we can get the hell out of this place for a while? Maybe today will be a relaxing day."

"Okay," an almost silent whine left her mouth.

They began to gather their belongings and head for the door. As Leena reached for the handle, it without warning started to shake, violently. Forcing them to jump a few feet back, they looked at each other, raised a brow and looked back at the door, which was no longer vibrating. Throwing the door open, a young, scared and shaking woman was standing just beyond the threshold. Tears streaming from her eyes, leaving a mascara stain on her cheeks.

"Bella!" Mark screamed, grabbing her arm as he pulled her lightly into his.

Slamming the door shut, Leena ran to the kitchen, dampened a rag, grabbed a glass of water, and rushed back to Mark. Helping the terrified Bella to the couch, he rubbed her back, holding her in his muscled arms. Placing soft kisses on her forehead, she was unable to get a word out, only sobs. Growing tired of the cries, Leena sat in front of

Bella, looked her in the eyes, forcing the young woman to relax.

"Bella?"

"Yes," she sniffled.

"What happened?" she kept her concentration.

"It's my mom," Bella cried.

"Your mom?" Leena placed her hand on Bella's for a stronger connection.

"She was taken! We were having a wonderful conversation. She was telling me about her sales for the day and how excited she was to decorate for the Coleman Fall Festival. He just crashed through the door, grabbed my mother, ripped into her neck and left me with a message!" she expressed; sorrow consumed her.

"Who? Bella, who was it? What was the message?" Leena slightly tightened her grip.

The tears stopped as Bella looked deep into Leena's eyes. Pulling her arm away from Leena, she reached into her purse, grabbed a pen and without warning, she quickly thrust it into her neck. Falling to the floor, blood pouring from her self-inflicted wound, Mark swiftly fell to his knees.

"Philip!" Bella choked on her blood; pen still lodged in her neck.

"No!" she screamed, pulling Bella close.

Removing the pen from her neck, Leena shoved it into her wrist. Gently placing her wrist to Bella's mouth, she saw her wound slowly heal and her breath was beginning to steady itself. Mark picked her up off the floor, walked to Leena's room and softly placed her on the bed.

"Son of a bitch!" Mark quietly expressed, exiting the room as he threw a pillow at the front door.

"Mark! Relax!" she made a feeble attempt to calm him down.

"No, he kidnapped Luna, tried to kill my girlfriend," he whispered.

"I'm aware, however we can't approach this halfcocked!"

"Maybe not, but he needs to be stopped, Leena," he was anxiously pacing around the room.

"I agree. If I am being honest, I don't believe it'll stop after Philip. I think our lives have just gotten complicated. If he was good at one thing, it was gathering followers, regardless of who or what they are!"

Hearing Bella in the room, he made his way to comfort her. Feeling unwelcomed stress, she placed a flask of Dr. Plasma in the microwave for a quick heat. Calling James, she begged for him and Matt to come over. Realizing her day was surely ruined, she slouched in her chair, rubbed her temples, awaiting the arrival of her partner. She was now sure that her best chance was to stay with Raphael. After all, if anyone had the means to protect her, it was the king. Roughly an hour had passed, when her cat nap was disturbed by a rapping at the door.

"Yeah!" she answered.

James and Matt entered the apartment, eyes widened as they witness the blood splattered floor, broken window, and overturned furniture. Sitting on the couch next to Leena, they looked around trying to figure out the mystery. Mark left the bedroom, waved at his friends, grabbed a beer from the fridge and sat on the floor. Silence once more filled the apartment as both Leena and Mark were left sighing deeply, rolling their eyes.

"Up to discuss what happened?" James eyed Leena.

"If you can't figure it out by looking, then maybe you're not meant to be a detective!" Leena tried to be sarcastic, but her remark was filled instead with bitchiness.

"Sorry, damn!" James looked away.

"James, it has just been an interesting night, carrying into today," Mark calmed the room down.

"All the more reason to update us."

"Last night, Leena spent some time alone with Raphael. He extended an invite for her to move above the bar. When she entered her apartment, she was attacked by Philip. Remembering I had left a spell book here, I made my way to pick it up. Thankfully, I made it in time, as I am quite sure Philip was close to ripping her heart out. Throwing him out of the window, we couldn't find any trace of him," Mark began to explain.

"Philip?"

"My brother."

"Wait, you have a brother?" James was struck with confusion.

"Never mind that," Mark spoke.

"And how did that lead into today?" Matt interjected.

"We were getting ready to head out when Bella showed up, banging on the door. We let her in, when once again all hell broke loose. She was compelled to relay a message and afterword's, kill herself, well attempt to, he obviously knew that Leena would save her," Mark finished.

"He said he was going to hurt me," Leena spoke, her words filled with attitude.

"What?" James was now sitting closer to Matt, finding comfort.

"When he was in the process of torturing me, Philip said that he was going to make my life a living hell. Summing it up in my own words of course."

"Has Captain Sommers been informed?" Matt pulled out a small pad with a pen attached to the side. To Leena, she felt as though Matt was trying a little too hard to impress the captain. He'd learn, it may take a while, but he'll learn. Lauren Sommers is your typical TV captain. She barked orders, left for meetings at random times, heartless, etc.

"No, and its staying that way!" Leena barked.

"Because?"

"Philip was, is a whiny brat. He will do everything he can to get his way. He stated he will make my life a living hell and I need to prepare myself for that! Not only will I have to deal with detective work, but I now get the joy of keeping everyone I hold close safe. He won't give up, that I can assure you," Leena chugged her Dr. Plasma. They spent the rest of the day making her apartment look somewhat normal again. Keeping their phones at the ready in case someone wanted to wreak havoc once again.

5

With no news on Luna and her whereabouts, Bella spent the next week and a half close to Mark, for safety and comfort. It was a roughly quiet week, no destruction or life threats from Philip. It felt like he was taking a break, like he needed to recharge. The morning sun filled the apartment as Leena stretched, kicking the blankets off the edge of the bed. Knowing her break has come to an end, she let out a long, tired sigh.

Placing her clothing out on the bed, she noticed her lack of variety. Her normal wardrobe consists of jeans, t-shirt, leather jacket and her combat boots. Never has she owned a pair of high heels in her life, hell she hasn't worn a skirt or dress. It just wasn't her. She hasn't seen the practicality of chasing someone in heels. Deciding she would try something new, she quickly showered, threw on her standard attire and stood at the counter, waiting for James. Scrolling through her phone, she looked at a few different outfits, shaking her head as nothing looked like proper detective wear. Her concentration was broken by a knock on the door.

"Morning!" James happily poked his head into the apartment.

"Hi," she smiled.

"Ready?"

"No, but really don't have a choice. It has been eerily quiet, and I've just been waiting for shit to hit the fan," she laughed to herself.

"Well its useless to sit and wait. We've been detectives long enough to know that," he made his way back to the car.

Leena looked around her apartment for a while, wondering how long it would take for her to move her things. Laughing to herself, she made her way to the parking garage. Seeing Matt in the front seat, she threw open the back door and climbed in. She checked herself out in the rearview mirror and lightly tapped Matt's shoulder, bidding him a good morning.

"How are you?" Matt smiled. He had such a bright smile, it truly lit up a room. He could almost get anyone to do anything by just smiling and letting his bright eyes do the talking.

"Stressed, irritated, the works."

The three friends pulled away from the building, inching into the busy morning traffic. Catching up on the week, they did everything they could to forget about the killer running loose. Passing the first sign indicating the direction of the police department, the radio began to ring.

"What can I do for you?" James pressed the answer button on his steering wheel.

"Enough with the small talk!" Captain Sommers barked into the phone. "There has been a murder at the Hillside Apartments. It was arson, that's all we know for now. Go!" Sommers bellowed, hanging up without so much as a goodbye or good luck.

"Arson! Really!" Leena began to bang her head against the window.

"To think, we thought it was going to be a delightful day back at the office," Matt allowed himself to laugh, but not for long.

"Looks like we are detouring," James sighed, irritation filling his voice.

As this was going to be Matt's first murder without a supervisor, he was rather excited. Sorrowful for the loss of life, he prepared himself, gathering his pen and notebook. Running his hands over his chest, ridding his newly purchased blazer of any wrinkles. The remainder of the car ride was filled with silence and the occasional mutter under one's breath. Leena looked up to see where they were when her trance was broken by her vibrating blazer pocket.

"Hi Raphe," Leena spoke without enthusiasm.

"What's up?"

"The usual, another day another murder. Heading to a case as we speak."

"What a way to bring in a work week," he laughed.

"You know, you could show a little bit of empathy for the dead!" her voice grew irritable.

"No, really, I can't," his laugh escalated. Hanging up the phone, she shook her head, cursed Raphael, and looked out the window. Seeing the apartments growing close, she saw smoke rising from the building.

6

The vehicle pulled up to the apartments, smoke still poured from the building. As they climbed out, they saw groups of people, families just standing on the other side of the road. Sadness and fear filled the air as people held their loved ones close. With the holidays approaching, Leena felt for these families. She felt it wrong to complain about her life when just moments ago, someone lost their life and people lost their homes.

As an officer lifted the tape, both Leena and James ducked under. Leaving Matt behind, who was now asking some of the bystanders if they knew of any information that would help with the case. A woman stood near a few officers who appeared to console her. She was tall, approximately 6'2". Her shirt fit her curves perfectly, not a large woman by any means. The woman's bosom looked as if it were trying to escape her shirt, her cleavage catching the attention of a few young men who happened to be passing by. Eyes, though they were filled with tears, were a beautiful green with a ring of yellow around the iris. Her green and gold speckled shirt brought attention to the beautiful, sorrow filled eyes.

The young woman ran a hand through her long, wavy, black hair as the other was wiping away the thickly applied mascara that was running down her face. Noticing that conveniently the bluecoats who were by the woman's side were rather young, Leena quickly waved them off. Walking up to the sobbing woman, she grabbed a tissue from one of the officers, handed it to the woman and waited patiently for the sobs and hiccups that accompanied to come to a halt. She sniffled for a moment, made eye contact with Leena, and calmed herself.

"Miss Thorne?"

"Megan, please," her sobbing wasn't as intense as it was moments ago.

"Megan, how well did you know the victim?" Leena asked, careful not to stir up emotions.

"He is... was my boyfriend!" the crying grew louder, leaving Leena to hold in her frustration. All she wanted was to get this over with.

"Why was he alone in the apartment?"

"We had a fight, he cheated on me with some bimbo from the gym!" she barked.

Megan's rant was quickly interrupted as Matt called for Leena, running in her direction. Tripping over his feet, he made quick contact with the ground. Growling in anger, he threw his fist at the grass. Rushing over to him, James knelt in front of him.

"Matt! Calm down!" he whispered, showing affection, forcing others to grow bored.

"I'm sorry," Matt's voice cracked.

"Babe? Have you been practicing control?" James helped him up, looking around being sure that everyone has moved on.

Before Matt had a chance to answer, Leena was marching in their direction. Annoyance filling her mind and irritation filled her eyes. Fearing the worst, James placed himself close to Matt, ready to defend him.

"What the hell was that about?" she tried to keep her voice down.

"Leena, relax, Matt is just happy to have his first case."

"Happy! Look, Matt, I am glad that you joined the force. However, this isn't something to be happy about, a man was burned to death in his apartment. You have to be professional, more than you have been," Leena helped him to brush off the dirt and grass.

"I'm really sorry."

"What do you have?" Leena grabbed the paper from his hand. Reading the notes that were scribbled on the paper, she looked up to Matt and over at James.

"The victim is Austin," her words were filled with confusion.

"Austin, Austin Hayes?" James was quick to grab the paper from her hand.

"I didn't think he was back," Leena spoke looking around the area.

"Hello! Who is Austin?" Matt interjected, waving his arms in an attempt to break their conversation.

"Mark's cousin, they were close, real close. He had more in common with him than he did with anyone. He wasn't a witch by birth, but he did practice. He worked for tech support at some huge chemical company down state. When Mark and Austin saw each other, which was rare, they would nerd out like crazy. Comic books, movies, TV, books, etc. Austin was more shamanistic than anything else, though he hardly tapped into his abilities."

"Well what the hell brought him back? Why didn't he contact us, or even Mark? James pondered.

"He did," a familiar voice forced them to spin around.

"Mark!"

"Hi, Leena," sorrow filled his voice.

Pushing his way through the officers and around Megan, who was once again being consoled by a young cop, made his way in Leena's direction. He looked gray, dull, like he hadn't slept in days. He pulled off his stained gloves, threw them in a bag that was being held by another medical examiner and fixed his blazer as he approached his friends. Unwilling to give his friends a hug as he wasn't the cleanest at the moment, he waved and forced a smile.

"Have you?" Leena questioned, pointing at the apartment complex.

"Been in there the whole time? Yeah," Mark interrupted his friend.

Completely disregarding his avoidance for a hug, she rushed over, throwing her arms around him. It forced Mark to bring his feelings forward. Tears began to well in his eyes and roll down his cheeks. Pulling away, he used the inside of his sleeve to wipe the tears away. He looked over to James and back at Leena, they stood in silence for a moment.

"How long have you been at the scene?" James asked.

"About thirty minutes more than you have. I was Austin's ICE contact, so I was the first to be called," Mark spoke, his voice still choked.

"Can you fill us in?"

"Better question is, can we get in? Take a look around?" Leena fixed her hair as she looked up to the shattered apartment window.

Mark began to nod his head as he gathered his thoughts, he went over to talk with Megan. Scooting by their friend, Leena, James, and Matt made their way into the lobby. Noticing the elevator was out of order and yellow tape enclosed the doors, they looked for Austin's floor. As he was near the top of the complex, they began to ascend the stairs. Floor by floor, the smell of smoke began to grow stronger. Filling their noses with dust and an unpleasant smell, the occasional sneeze would fill the silent hallways. The air felt heavier as they approached Austin's apartment level.

As the others were focused on the charred walls, Leena felt a familiar presence. Allowing James to lead the group, she walked up to the next level. Rounding the next set of stairs, she saw Raphael standing in the corner. Feeling like he was in the shadows just to startle her, she shook her head. Raphael stood tall, tanned, and chiseled. His muscles rippled under his long sleeve thermal undershirt, she could see the outline of his biceps, she felt weak in the knees. He was one of the few men that made her feel this way. Her eyes widened as she noticed a change in Raphael's appearance, he had dyed his hair, dark blonde to be exact. She liked it.

"Nice," Leena pointed at his head.

"Yeah, wanted to change it up a bit. Thinking I will keep it," he spoke, walking in her direction.

Her focus was now drawn to his chest as his pectorals attempted to tear through his shirt. Leena could clearly identify each muscle, it seemed as though Raphael had no body fat. As he closed in, she placed her hand on his chest. Realizing that she was at work, she quickly removed her hand, pushing him away. His face was soon filled with a smile as he knew he had won this battle of lust.

"I need to get back to work," Leena turned away, speaking softly.

"So be it. I'll be waiting for you at Eternal Night."

A quick kiss on her forehead and he was gone. She looked around, the walls blackened by smoke and the floor covered in soot. The apartments were ghostly, it felt as though death had claimed the building for itself. She made her way through the door, both James and Matt now eyeing her curiously.

"Shouldn't you be working?" Leena barked, looking around the scorched apartment.

"Maybe. How's Raphael?" James chuckled.

"What makes you think I was talking to him."

"Well, your breath grew heavy, your eyes lit up like the sky on the fourth of July and when you came in here, you had an ear-to-ear grin," Matt spoke, using his pen to flip over a few burned papers on what use to be a desk.

After some time in the apartment, Mark appeared through the door with Megan quickly following behind. Her height forcing her to duck to get through the door, she once again began to weep. Megan made her way to the bedroom, again leaving the team alone.

"What did you two talk about?" Leena walked over to her friend.

"Found out she was in the apartment. She walked in on Austin cheating. Megan threw the woman out and the two of them got into it. According to some neighbors it was pretty heated."

"Pretty heated," Leena put her hands up, putting her words in quotations as she looked around the room.

"What is that supposed to mean?" Megan exited the bedroom, glaring at Leena.

"All I'm saying is that we shouldn't rule out all possibilities," she looked over to Mark, giving him the "this could be supernatural" glance.

Quickly recognizing Leena's gesture, Mark slowly led Megan out of the apartment. As they were leaving the room, Megan looked back toward Leena, glaring, whispering under her breath. Her eyes widened as she tried to make out the whispered words.

"James!" she smacked his shoulder, keeping her shout as quiet as possible.

"What?"

"I think she might have had something to do with Austin's murder!"

"What are you talking about?" his eyes rolled in annoyance, showing a bit of anger.

"Mark couldn't find any source of intentional arson, right? Well maybe that is because it could have been spontaneous, human combustion," Leena looked around the apartment.

"People don't just burst into flames, Leena, give it a rest!" Matt put his opinion in, forcing an evil eyed look from his friend.

"Fine, then why did she lie about being in the apartment? I'm just saying that we should get her down to the precinct and ask a few questions, that is all," she shook her head, holding in her anger towards Matt. Leena knew he was trying to make life easier on her, but she couldn't help but feel like something was really off.

Matt grabbed James by the hand leading him out of the apartment. Leaving Leena alone, she looked around, allowing a deep sigh to leave her lungs. The apartment was still filled with the smell of smoke and burnt flesh. The afternoon was coming to an end and Leena was growing tired of the rancid odors filling her nasal cavities. After spending hours talking to the families and friends that were stranded outside the apartment complex, Leena made her way to the morgue. With snow beginning to fall, bystanders began to bring hoodies and blankets out to the ones in need. Some even allowed others to be brought into their homes.

7

Pulling into the parking spot in front of the building, she slowly climbed out of the taxi she was forced to call. Tossing some cash on the driver's lap, she smiled, stretched, and made her way through the double glass doors. Placing her gun, badge, and wallet on the x-ray tray, she slid it across the bars. Standing under the tall body scanner, Leena waited patiently for the beep of approval, indicating confirmation of passage. Looking across the hall through the small window on the swinging door, she saw Mark's head bobbing up and down. He was waiting, impatiently.

"Leena!" he plowed through the doors, wrapping his arm over her shoulders.

"Anxious, are we?"

"What? No! Maybe," he bounced up and down.

"What the hell has you so wired?"

"After I wrapped up the conversation with Megan, I came to the morgue to examine what I could of the remains. Been a long day, lots of coffee and energy drinks!" he continued to bounce down the hall.

"Mark? Can I ask you something?" Leena quietly asked, looking around the dimly lit hallway.

"Yeah, yeah, yeah," his mouth spat out the rushed words.

"Why were you so close with Megan? You don't know her and yet it felt like you were defending her," she stopped mid stride, looking at her friend.

"Defending? I wasn't defending her! I just refused to listen to you call her my cousins' killer! The first person that's questioned at the scene isn't always the criminal!" he barked, ignoring her pause, he kept walking.

"Mark! Come on! You know that's not what I meant. I'm just saying that you warmed up to her a little fast!" Leena rushed up to be by his side.

Opening the doors to the unnecessarily bright room, Leena could smell the various odors that typically accompany a medical lab, bleach, formaldehyde, and other solvents, which created an assault on the senses. She looked over to the table where she witnessed the ashes of Austin Hayes scattered across the surface. Walking up to the operating table, she hovered her hand over the remains. Feeling angered, but mostly sadness for Mark, she clenched her fist, closed her eyes for a moment of silence and made her way to the desk. Sliding the stool away from the table, she saw a few abnormal sketches and random notes on his tablet.

"Mark!" she grabbed his attention. "What's this?" Leena was now pointing at the notebook.

"Yeah! Oh," his voice echoed through the room, dying down as soon as he realized what she was looking at.

"Explain? Now!" Leena's voice went from calm and collected to quickly growing irritable.

"I'm confident that you need to get some sleep! I don't know what the hell is going on with you, but you have got to stop freaking out every time you turn a corner or flip open a folder! They're just markings, notes, things I keep for myself. Sometimes I doodle on my notebook when I have a mental roadblock at work, or I just can't seem to focus! What is your goddamn problem?" Mark punched the pillar, controlling his anger.

Throwing the notebook at her friend, she looked him deep in the eyes. Ignoring the shocked expression on his face, Leena walked away from the table, leaned against a pillar, and ran her hand through her hair. Disregarding his friend, Mark walked back over to the table, once again examining the ashes. Leena began to unexplainably grow more and more angry with every tick of the clock.

She looked up, eyes growing dark. Losing control of her actions, she charged at Mark. Without hesitation, he spun on his heels while simultaneously snapping his fingers. A wave of yellow energy emanated from his core. Striking Leena with the force of a 4x4 fully loaded pickup truck, she was thrown across the room, slamming hard against the far wall. Seemingly lifeless on the floor, she was engulfed in a small cloud of energy.

He slowly walked up to Leena, stood by her side, waiting for her to wake up. Feeling like he may have put a bit too much force into his spell, he paced around for a long while, hours even. Time passed, her body clenched, and she snapped back to reality. Gasping for air, she jumped to her feet, placed her hand on Mark's shoulder and gathered her stability.

"The full moon is getting close and the werewolf in you really wants to come out and play," Mark pulled himself from her hands.

"What?"

"Your first full moon as a hybrid. This Friday, the 23rd is the full moon. It'll be the first time your body wants to transition to full on wolf. As that is not possible considering you're a hybrid, you will just grow to be hateful and angry. So, with the day growing close, you should probably learn to control your urges and feelings."

"I'm sorry," a sorrowful expression filled her face as pain filled her eyes.

"Don't be sorry, you're not an apologetic person, just control yourself, okay!" he lightly tapped her shoulder, slowly making his way to his desk.

Anger still boiled through Leena's blood, choosing to ignore the hate growing inside her, she limped over to the vending machine, slid a few coins into the slot and punched in a number. Growling to life, the machine lightly shook, dropping a flask of room temperature Dr. Plasma. Leena popped open the drink letting out a long sigh. Watching Mark pace around the ashes, she once again broke the silence, pulling a piece of drywall from her hair.

"Mark?"

"Yup!"

"I'm going to say something; I want you to try your hardest to not get overly defensive. Okay?" she chugged the Dr. Plasma, tossing aside the flask.

"What is it?" Mark was focused, determined to find Austin's killer.

"When you and Megan left the apartment earlier, she turned back to me, whispered something and continued on her way. As she turned back towards you, I saw a mark just behind her right ear. It was the Roman Numeral for the number nine. I only bring this up because your tablet had a few random drawings, each of them had that symbol incorporated. Did you know that?"

"Like I said, they are random, they just happen, I doodle."

"Do you think maybe you connected with Megan more than you thought?" Leena weaseled carefully around the sentence.

"What are you trying to say?"

"Well, you're tired. This case has you all over the place. Maybe your mental walls aren't functioning properly."

"You're telling me that you think she got in my head?" his brow lifted, and lips pursed.

"Maybe, I mean it could explain it. However small the chances are, it's possible."

Mark shook his head, getting his thoughts back into his work. The evening took them by storm, before Leena could realize how long she had been at the morgue the clock chimed. Indicating that yet another hour had passed, she checked her phone.

"Seven! Where the hell did the day go?"

"Time flies when your dead!" Mark laughed a little too hard, forcing him to hold his sides. "Yeah, you've been here for a while. Talking, attacking me, laying on the ground passed out."

"Yeah! I get it!" she rubbed a finger over the goose egg on her head.

Leena gave up on the day, deciding to make her way to Eternal Night. Helping Mark to pack up a few of his belongings, she whipped out her phone, called a taxi and ordered yet another ride. Eventually she was going to get a car, only to mix with the rest of society. She never really felt it necessary to own a vehicle as she always had a ride, not to mention with her speed she could be anywhere in town within a blink of an eye. Most of the time anyway. Allowing herself to be smothered by an abnormally long hug from her dear friend, she chose to return the hug. Seldom showing affection to anyone, she would always make an exception for Mark, no matter how big of an argument they had. Leaving the morgue, she climbed into the taxi, rolled down the window as Mark leaned against the door. Ending their conversation and bidding each other farewell for the night, Leena handed a card with Eternal Nights address, subtly informing the taxi driver where she wanted to go.

"Night!"

"Night, Mark!" she waved as the taxi pulled away, drove over a speed bump, and pulled out into the speeding Coleman traffic.

8

The taxi whipped into the parking lot across from the bar. Looking up to the many windows, she saw very few lights on, indicating the small chances of Raphael being home. With the snow continuing to fall, she looked around, guessing that there was a possibility of at least eight inches blanketing the Earth. Handing the driver a twenty-dollar bill, she declined the change, threw on her jacket as she made her way to the doors. She stood for a moment in the empty room, chairs on tables and dim lights hung over the stage.

"Alone, finally!" she expressed, throwing her hands in the air, joy filling her emotions.

Feeling her way through the bar, she made her way around the counter, mixed a drink, pulled down a stool and kicked her feet up to the counter. Rocking the chair, the silence was occasionally filled with the creaking of the stool legs. Her drink was short lived as she downed the last few drops. Leena placed the glass in the sink, turned towards the stairwell, flicked on the light for the attic room and hopped up the stairs.

Happily throwing her clothing on the floor, Leena made her way to the bath. Filling the tub with warm water, she threw in some lavender essential oils, bath bubbles and lit an unscented candle. The room quickly filled with a wonderful, relaxing scent. Inhaling deeply, she stepped lightly into the tub, knelt down and slowly leaned against the tub wall. The bubbles covered her body, flowing gently over her bosom, leaving only her neck and head exposed.

Time passed and relaxation was still present. She dipped her long, wavy, brown hair into the water, allowing the essential oils to soften her now wet curls. Holding her breath, she lowered herself under the water for a moment, allowing the water to wash over her, cleansing her aura. Coming up for a breath, Leena sat for a moment, rung out her hair, grabbed a towel and placed herself in front of the mirror. Flashing lights would occasionally fill the room as cars passed by outside, small chatter would flow through the closed windows from young kids playing around across the street.

Leena's gaze was broken as the door to the room was slowly pushed open, hinges squeaking eerily. Turning around, she witnessed a tall silhouette standing in the doorway. Unable to make out who it was as a light behind the figure made it unrecognizable. Holding her towel in place with one hand, she clenched the other into a tight fist, ready to defend. She wasn't in the mood to fight wrapped in a towel, but if she had to, she would.

"Leena, what brings you here my love?" a deep, growling voice took over the room.

"Raphe?" her hand relaxed.

Walking from the shadows, he smiled, kicked off his boots and inched closer to the beautiful, half naked woman in his room. Leena stood, frozen in place. Looking deep into Raphael's hazel eyes, her knees began to weaken, her breath grew heavy.

Why? How is he one that makes me feel this weak? Leena thought to herself, eyeing Raphael as he continued to inch closer.

Placing his hand on her waist, he looked down, meeting her radiant eyes, leaned in for a kiss. Leena closed her eyes, allowing Raphael to hold her in place as she felt her knees would no longer do the job. She felt his breath on her skin and soon after the contact of his warm lips connected with hers. Dropping the towel, she quickly kicked it to the side as he picked her up, wrapped her legs around his waist and in an ecstasy filled moment she threw her head back exposing her neck. Looking each other in the eyes, they smiled.

Still holding Leena in his muscle-bound arms, he placed his forehead on hers, indicating passion and love. Pulling Leena away from his body, he tossed her on the bed. Pulling off his t-shirt, he leaned over Leena who began to unfasten his belt and undo the button on his jeans. Ripping the jeans away from his body, she grabbed his firm, muscular glutes. Feeling the muscles move under her hands, she let out a deep sigh, grasping tighter, lightly biting Raphael's neck. Forcing him to growl, arousal filled the room and lust filled their eyes.

Flipping Raphael on his back, she slowly climbed on top, settling herself on his waist. Looking down on Raphael, Leena's lips cracked a smile. She hadn't felt this way in years, hundreds of years to be more accurate. Leena herself would go so far as to say a thousand years. Raphael smiled back to the beautiful woman, grabbed the back of her head, and pulled her close. He didn't dare to kiss her, only gaze into her eyes where they sat for a moment. No passion, no sensual acts, only the sheer energy of love flowing between them. Allowing the moments of sexual tension to grow, they soon gave in to their urges. Filling the night with desire and the mixed fragrance of musk and the radiant floral scent that Leena donned, her signature homemade body oil. A beautiful mix of orange blossom, honey, and patchouli, she called it, The Pharaohess.
With the night quickly giving way to the morning hours, Leena gently placed her head on Raphael's chest. Hearing his slow, calm, almost nonexistent heartbeat, her eyes began to flutter and grow heavy. The room was filled with a soft snore emanating from Raphael, who quickly fell asleep. Another smile grew across Leena's face, she ran her hand across his chest, allowing the call of sleep to consume her.

"Morning bitch!" a recognizable voice pierced her ears.

"Shit!"

"Just the reaction I was hoping for."

Leena turned over, eyes connecting with her brothers. Her pulse quickened, breath grew heavy and though she didn't believe it could happen, her palms began to sweat. Yet another delightful side effect of being a hybrid, she was still getting used to being "alive" again. Philip's eyes filled with hate and the desire to kill, he lunged toward Leena. Attempting to move out of the way, she rolled off the bed, falling on her back. Facing her murderous brother, she quickly tried to crawl away. Pain filled her mind, her body as Philip drove his hand deep into her back. Grabbing her spine, he pulled, leaving Leena to wince in pain.

Ripping herself away, she was quickly dragged back to reality. Looking around the loft, she began to slowly realize that it was just a dream. With a quickened breath, Leena rolled on her back, looked up to the ceiling and filled the room with a long, deep sigh. Hearing the shower, she looked over to see no sign of Raphael next to her. Throwing on her clothing, she made her way downstairs, placed a coffee pod in the machine, pressed brew and filled the main floor with the soft smell of steamed coffee grounds.

9

Leena paced around the bar, coffee in her hands. She could still hear the sound of running water making its way through the pipes. Placing a stool on the floor, she slowly sat, kicked her feet up and continued to sip the coffee. The sun filled the room, casting shadows over the floor. She grabbed the remote, clicked the play button and listened as the radio roared to life.

Music filled the room. Looking up to the clock, Leena saw she still had time before she needed to make her way to the precinct. Noticing the silence within the walls, she saw Raphael's shadow dancing down the stairs. Mocking Leena's previous actions, he made a rather large cup of coffee, sat across from Leena, and smiled.

"Morning!" he winked.

"Enjoy your shower?"

"It could've been better with company," Raphael nudged Leena's leg under the table.

She smiled, ear to ear. Looking around the room, she was interrupted as the doorbell buzzed. Allowing Raphael to finish his coffee, she made her way to the door. With a swift motion, she pushed the doors open, filling the room with light and a cold winters breeze. Rubbing her hands along her arms in an attempt to warm herself, she saw no one standing outside. Looking around, she saw a package addressed to her sitting just before her feet. Bringing the package to the table, Leena gently placed it in front of Raphael. Inspecting the package, he ran a finger across the tape.

"Is this from you?" Leena raised a brow. "Since when do you do gifts?"

"Nope," he continued to chug his coffee. "And I have given gifts before, you'd be surprised!"

Shooting an evil glance in his direction, Leena shook her head with a hint of irritation. Taking a knife from the other side of the counter, she slid it across the tape. The box popped open with force after being tightly taped over. Raphael walked over to make himself another cup of coffee as Leena pulled the box tabs to the side.

"Shit!" Leena stumbled back, tripping over a chair. Connecting hard with the floor.

Quickly rushing to Leena's side, he gave her a once over, making sure she wasn't wounded. It wasn't something he needed to do, but this was just another way to show how loving and caring he could be. They slowly stood up, fixed her wrinkled clothing, and stood for a moment. Raphael looked to Leena; confusion filled his eyes.

"What the hell was that about?"

"Look for yourself," she pointed to the box. "I'll give you a single guess as to who it was."

"Philip?" the name fell from his mouth with disgust.

Raphael pulled down two tabs of the box, leaned over and without a beat he covered his nose, pulling himself away. Holding her breath, Leena walked back up to the box. Filled with rage, she pulled out the severed head of an unknown man. Placing it on the table, she dug through the box, pulled her hand out, revealing an envelope. Leena shook her head, showing how disinterested she was in opening the letter.

"I really don't think you have a choice in whether you read it or not," he placed a hand against her back. "Should I?" he questioned, giving Leena an out.

"No! I'll do it," Leena pulled away. "How bad can it be? Philip said he was going to make my life a living hell. There is no reason to be shocked by anything he does."

"I'll be right here," he pushed the box to the side, almost knocking the severed head to the floor.

Ripping open the letter, she threw the blood-stained envelope on the floor. Letter in hand, a small amount of blood dripped from the corner of the paper. She could still make out the words, unsettling words.

"Leena, happy birthday to me. I hope you enjoyed my present to you. Good luck finding the body, as a courteous heads up I'll be killing another innocent person today if the body to your gift isn't found within the next 12 hours. With great hatred, The Darkest Rose."

"Psychotic," Raphael began to shake his head. "If he weren't trying to kill you, I may just like this kid."

Throwing the letter back in the box, she glared at Raphael. Knowing all too well what the look meant, he quickly fell silent. Pacing around, she continued to every so often glance over to the clock.

"10 a.m., I'm already going to be late for work!"

"You can take my car; I will deal with this."

"Thanks, but things will only get worse if I don't deal with it. I'm not overly excited about dealing with more than one murder today."

"Hey, you don't know if you have a lot of work or not! Go in, see what you have to deal with and work on this case in the back of your mind."

"It would just be so much easier if Captain Sommers could be informed!"

"Why can't she? Maybe if she is in the know, she can lighten your load a little bit," he smiled. "She took the position knowing all too well what it would entail."

Nodding her head, indicating that she had given into his idea, she gathered her few belongings, stole the keys from Raphael's hand and kicked open the doors. Leaving her lover behind to clean up her psychopathic brother's mess, she sat for a few moments in his car. The sun tried to peek through the clouds, but the fall weather as usual disapproved of the sun giving life to the ground. Snow once again began to lightly dust the windshield of the car; windows grew fogged over as the vehicle was heating up. Leena looked to the digital clock on the dashboard.

"10:30," Leena sighed, knowing she was late, later than usual. Slapping the gearshift into drive, she pulled away from Eternal Night. Ignoring stop signs and lights, she sped off to the Coleman Police Department. Her focus was broken, shifting to her phone as it blared out the phone companies' signature basic ringtone.

"James!"

"An hour! You're an hour late. Captain Sommers has been asking for you!" James screamed, his voice almost rupturing her eardrum. "Where are you?"

"I'm barreling towards you as we speak. Had a little birthday surprise from Philip."

"Philip!" her eardrums were once again close to rupturing. "We haven't dealt with him in a while! Captain needs to know."

"Shut the hell up! As far as we know Captain Sommers has no idea what, or who he is. I don't need a game of 20 questions when I arrive at work!" she returned the ear splitting, headache inducing scream.

"Well what happened?"

"It's Philip's birthday today and I was the one to receive a gift."

"Which was?"

"A severed head in a box. He decided that I had the day to discover the body. If I don't find the body in twelve hours, he will kill again," her tone steady and very nonchalant.

"What time did you open the box?"

"Just before ten, I'm guessing he probably killed, wrote the note and dropped off the present around nine this morning."

Leena's drive continued to be filled with questions and the occasional awkward sigh. Any other person on this planet would have hung up the phone, Leena knew better.

James may have just been fey, but oh boy, if you piss him off it will feel like you've gone up against a rabid wolverine. She would personally choose to go up against Matt as a werewolf, he'd be less terrifying. Hell, Philip would be a better choice.

Noticing that she hasn't seen a mile marker in quite some time, she tossed the phone on the passenger seat, knowing James would grow bored and end the call. You can only talk so long to yourself before you realize you might be crazy. Miles and miles passed and with great concentration, Leena saw that she had yet to pass a sign.

What the hell? She thought to herself, looking left and right. I hate when James calls and begins a rant, I had to have taken a wrong turn. Her thoughts began to grow as signs didn't present themselves.

Pulling off to the side of the road, she twisted the key, listening as the car died down, she sat staring off into the woods. A sick feeling began to boil in her stomach, peering across the street she felt a familiar feeling. Leena's eyes grew about twice their normal size, her hands grew clammy and a bead of sweat formed above her brow. Stepping out of the car, she soon realized that she was on Old 10, the street that leads to Claresville. Not only did she get detoured, but she was right next to Claresville Forest.

"Shit!" Leena kept her voice as quiet as possible. "How the hell did I get here?"

Leena quickly twisted the key once again. The engine clicked and turned over, unwilling to start. Punching the steering wheel, she leaned forward, placed her head on the wheel and sighed, deeply. Knowing from this point to the Coleman Police Department was another hour drive, she gave in to the unfortunate realization that she probably wasn't going to make it work.

"Captain is going to kill me!" Leena ran her hand through her hair, the wind through the windows knotting and twisting it with each movement.

Calling the Claresville Police Station, she paced around her car, waiting for the poor officer that got stuck with phone duty. The afternoon cold was beginning to settle in, checking the trunk for a jacket, she came up empty handed. Growing irritable, an equally irritated voice echoed through the phone.

"Claresville Police Station, Officer Hamson speaking."

"Detective Rose, Coleman Police Department. I am, well I was friends with Chief Samuel Blackhorn, I worked with him a few months back. I need escort, car broke down. I'm on Old 10, by Claresville Forest."

"We'll send a cruiser your way. Approximately fifteen minutes."

With that, the officer hung up the phone. Leaning against the car, she tilted her head back, shivers climbed up her spine. Her quivering brought to a swift halt as a shadow in the woods caught her attention. Without a thought, she barreled into the woods. Dodging limb after limb and leaping over logs of fallen trees, Leena stopped roughly fifty feet into the forest. Looking up into the canopy, she quickly dialed the Claresville Police Station.

"Claresville Police."

"Yeah, it's Detective Rose again!" Leena interrupted. "You might want to send a few more officers and call the Claresville Coroner, we've got a body in the woods."

Placing the phone back in her pocket, she walked back to the road, leaving a trail. Hopping onto the hood of her car, she leaned against the windshield, awaiting the arrival of the cruiser and backup officers. Minutes passed, though they felt like hours with the way the snow was beginning to fall. Somehow, Leena had no idea why, but the fog was still capable of clinging to the ground.

10

The long minutes passed when the silence of winter was broken by the sound of wailing sirens. Sliding off the hood of her car, she shook the snow from her hair, waved down the oncoming vehicles and stood patiently near the side of the road. Being careful to avoid any ice that formed, she paced around, waiting for the emergency vehicles to unload their equipment.

"Leena!"

"Samuel?" the deep, familiar voice forced her to spin around. She was happy, yes, but that didn't go unaccompanied. Her next few words were riddled with irritation. "Is that you?"

A tall, tanned and ruggedly handsome man began to approach her. His deep brown eyes accompanied with a charming smile and bulging biceps would be quick to grab anyone's attention. With each step the man took, his muscular pecs seemed to bounce, his hair moving with the wind. Growing closer to Leena, she could see his muscles struggling to stay inside his blue, button down shirt. The button slits almost stretched to the max.

Now standing toe to toe with Leena, he looked her deep in the eyes. Shaking her head back and forth, she gave in, looked him up and down, studying his choice in clothing. A few beats passed leaving her to give in to her feelings. Lunging towards him, she flung her arms around his shoulders, pulling him close. Unwilling to release him from the hug, Leena was struck with a sudden realization, forcing her to do so.

"What the hell!" she shoved him away, forcing him to reach for anything to help him keep his balance on the slippery road. "Why are you here?"

"Well, you see, I."

"No, No! I need to focus; your disappearing act is really the last thing I need on my mind! You can't just leave without a word and come back to treat everything as if it hasn't changed. You left without so much as farewell or kiss my ass," Leena pushed Samuel once more to the side, forcing him to give an angered glance.

Turning her back to Samuel, she trudged through the snow, forcing the emergency team to follow. The flakes began to grow, visibility into the woods was almost nonexistent. The tracks behind the team seemed to quickly disappear as thick snow continued to pile on the forest floor. Approaching the tree, Leena saw a few spots of red scattered over the ground.

"There," Leena waved her arm. "Over there."

"Don't see anything," an officer answered.

"Look up!"

A few officers gasped as others, including the medical examiner, looked up. Some hands placed on hips as other bluecoats took off their hats, in respect for the fellow officer. Growing angry with each passing second, she whipped out her phone.

"James!" she barked hindering him from speaking first.

"What?"

"I'm going to be late, extremely late. Philip is smart, I'll give him that."

"What happened?" his voice irritable.

"You know that present from this morning?" she turned from the group, being sure to keep her voice low. "I found the rest of it in Claresville Forest. Philip definitely is one crafty son of a bitch, placing the body in a different city would hinder anyone from Coleman finding it. If it weren't for your rant earlier, I may not have even wound up here."

"You're welcome, I guess."

"But there is one thing that has me questioning this whole thing," she spoke softly, taking a few steps away.

"Which is?"

"How convenient it was that Raphael's car broke down here."

"Maybe it was the vehicles time. I can't imagine him taking care of things."

"No, this feels different. Almost like someone was helping, like they were watching over me. There were no lights indicating things needed to be changed."

"Don't think much of it, okay?"

With that, James hung up the phone, leaving Leena to stand in the cold. Doing everything she can to keep warm, she was quickly called over by the Claresville Coroner. Being careful to not slip, Leena slowly climbed over a stump. The smell of death and decay filled her sinuses, forcing her to pull her shirt over her nose.

"What!" her question filled more with irritation than concern for the dead.

"This is Officer Mills, Jerry Mills. Very well known here in Claresville. Cause of death, decapitation."

"Gee, you think?" Leena filled the air with sarcasm. "I know exactly where the head is, long story. I'll have it brought to the morgue."

"Thank you!" with that, the medical examiner continued his work.

Gathering her thoughts, she once again found herself on her phone sending a quick message to Raphael. Alerting the examiner that the severed head should arrive within a few hours, she took this chance to head back up to the road. Watching Raphael's car as it was being loaded to the chains of the local tow truck. Looking around the unplowed, snow covered road, Leena saw Samuel finish a conversation with a rookie bluecoat and make his way in her direction. She tried to ignore him, a failed attempt of course.

"You okay?" she questioned genuinely.

"I am, yes. The rest of the team, I doubt they will be. What the hell did this?"

"Would you believe me if I told you it was Philip?"

"No!"

"Well believe it."

"Why did he do this?" Samuel pointed to the headless body being dragged from the woods. "What does he get out of it?"

"Torture me, kill innocent people and make my life a living hell. That would be my guess. He attacked me a couple weeks ago, almost killed me. If it weren't for Mark, I'd probably be dead."

"So, he's only back to torment and blackmail you?"

"Long story short, yes!"

"Leena, I really am sorry for the disappearing act," he rubbed her shoulders gently.

Inhaling deeply, she couldn't help but to partially believe him. She knew she cared for him, but she also cared for Raphael. Something she would never admit out loud, not yet anyway. Samuel pulled her close, the warmth of his body brought comfort to her. Looking him in the eyes, she placed a soft kiss to his lips. The other units had long gone and in her mind, she knew she was in the clear. Climbing into the back of Samuel's cruiser, he placed a jacket under Leena's head for support. Ripping the clothing from their bodies, Leena pulled Samuel in. Feeling him enter, she sighed with great ecstasy. The throbbing of Samuel had Leena in another world, a world free of worry, something that as of current only Raphael could do. The car windows grew fogged as moaning filled the air. After moments of pure lust, Leena and Samuel sat in the car, fixing their hair, and tossed on their clothing, exchanging glances of happiness.

They spent a moment catching up on Philip's more recent endeavors and Samuel's time, however short lived, spent in Missouri. With the afternoon cold beginning to settle in, both Leena and Samuel agreed it was time to get a move on. Before heading to the Claresville Police Station, they chose to stop for a quick cup of coffee. Climbing into their separate vehicles, one of which she borrowed from the Claresville precinct, Leena followed him into town, snow making travel next to impossible. As the city limits came into view, Leena noticed that Claresville never seemed to change, it was the dull city it always has been.

11

Pulling up to the Claresville Police Station, Leena pulled her car behind Samuels. Flashing his badge to the patrolmen, he was granted access with Leena as his guest. Stepping through the rotating doors, Leena's attention was caught by a room filled with men and women, cuffed to the various benches lining the walls. Making their way to the front desk, where a rather large man was shoving a doughnut in his face, her focus was drawn away by the ringing of her pocket.

"What?" Leena spoke, unwilling to deal with James and his annoyance. "I'm still in Claresville, I'll be back after I answer a few questions."

"I'm actually not calling to yell. I'm calling because Megan decided to show up with some information."

"Anything of interest?" Leena and Samuel continued through the double doors, passing the large guard behind the desk.

"Shockingly, yes, I really think you should hear this. It's information on Austin and his return."

"I can't leave, I found the body. You know the protocol."

"Guess I'll just take down any information I feel important."

With that, she hung up the phone. Following Samuel like a lost puppy, they arrived at the office. Simultaneously sitting at the desk, Leena waited for the questioning to begin. Moments crawled by when an irritated, properly dressed woman placed coffee and a flask of Dr. Plasma in front of them. Pulling out a battered, broken down chair, the woman gently placed herself in the seat.

Without a word, she studied Leena. Looking her up and down, she was careful to keep Leena in her view. As vampires killed Captain Jordyn's family, she was quite leery of anything magic, supernatural, or undead. For someone who is supposed to be an authoritative, levelheaded figure, Victoria Jordyn really had a hard time controlling her feelings.

"Samuel, care to explain the events of this morning? Seems like everyone feels as though I need to be kept out of the loop."

"Captain, how am I to know who calls what in? Dispatch sent my team and I the information, so we went."

"Doesn't seem too fair to keep a beheading from your captain now does it?"

"Fair!" Leena couldn't hold in her irritation any longer. "A fair is where you go to ride on rides, eat sugar coated food, waste money on rigged games and step in horse shit! You're a Captain, a rather shitty one at that!"

Shocked at Leena's sudden outburst, Captain Jordyn jumped from her seat. Angered, Samuel pulled Leena away from the table to the hallway. With a hand resting on her shoulder, he waited for Leena to steal a few deep breaths.

"Are you calm?"

"I am not going to sit there and have some mortal judge me! I didn't kill her damn family, and I sure as hell am not going to tell her that Philip was the one who killed her officer!"

"What if you did?"

"That's the same thing that Raphael asked," Leena looked him deep in the eyes. "If I tell anyone that Philip is the one raising extra hell on Earth, he will make things worse for me, for everyone!"

"Then what do you intend on doing?"

Ignoring his question, they noticed Captain Jordyn was once again sitting at the desk. Heading back to their chairs, Leena saw Captain Jordyn began to grow defensive. Almost as if she thought Leena was going to attack. Disregarding her annoying, protective gesture, Leena slowly sat in the chair, looked to Samuel, and rolled her eyes.

"Can we get on with a few questions?" Captain Jordyn clicked her pen as she flipped open her small notepad.

"Be my guest," Leena filled her words with sarcasm. "It isn't like I have anywhere to be."

"When you stumbled upon the body, was there anything out of the ordinary?" Leena rolled her eyes at the question. It had a clearly obvious answer; Captain Jordyn was just being her usual bitchy self.

"You mean other than the fact it was missing a head!" Leena couldn't help but answer with sarcasm, and a little irritation.

"His name is Jerry Mills, Detective Rose! Answer my question?"

"No, there wasn't anything in the area that struck me to be cautious. I saw the body, called the station and patiently waited for Samuel and his team."

"Was there a reason you requested Samuel to be on the scene?" she spoke, placing the tip of the pen in her mouth.

"She didn't request me, I was shockingly free," Samuel spoke, slouching in his chair without a care in the world.

"Detective Blackhorn, please? I will get to you later."

"Detective?" Leena cocked her head, looking toward Samuel, confusion filled her eyes. "What happened to Chief Blackhorn? And why did you lie about it?"

"Cut my status to stay here in Michigan. Didn't want you to think any less of me."

"Dumbass," Leena whispered. "As I said, I didn't request Samuel, hell I didn't even know he was fully back in town until today."

With the growing realization that she wasn't going to get any answers she wanted, Captain Jordyn closed the notebook and tucked the pen into her breast pocket. Displeased with the inability to frame Leena for Officer Mills death, she walked away, shaking her head. Any chance Victoria Jordyn had to put a supernatural behind bars, she took it. Her hatred fueled her work.

"So, Detective Blackhorn?"

"Yeah, I feel good about my choice. It allows me to be close to you, to be more involved in cases."

"Your choice, not mine. What makes you think we will be closer together?"

"You're only one town over."

"Do you really think that after the way you disappeared, we would go back to the old days? To the way things were?" Leena raised a brow, gazing deep into Samuels eyes. "Yeah we just fucked, but I didn't plan on giving into you."

"I plan on fighting like hell to get you to trust me again!"

"Well I wish you luck on that, Samuel. With everything going on right now, I doubt I could have anytime to even think of being with someone!"

"But you can sleep with Raphael? Yeah I know!" he grew angered. "Like he is any good for you!"

Her eyes grew dark, her fists clenched. Anger filled Leena to the brim. She knew important work drew him back to Missouri, but the least he could've done was allow Leena a proper goodbye. Looking away from him, Samuel took the gesture as a hint and stepped away. Alone in the musky, humid office, Leena saw through the blinds of Captain Jordyn's office. She was scolding Samuel, hands flying through the air, facial muscles tightened, and Leena would be damned if she didn't see steam erupt from her ears.

Exiting the dimly lit office, Samuel jerked his head towards the conference room. Understanding what that meant, Leena followed, slowly. Doing her best to pass the Captain's office undetected, she was sure to keep a watchful eye on Victoria. Reaching the large, chilly, and unsettling conference room, Leena braced herself against the wall.

"So?" Leena spoke, resting against the far corner of the room. "What happened?"

"I'm being transferred," a sigh left Samuel's mouth.

"You really pissed her off that bad?"

"Nope, according to her, she has no room for supernatural beings in her precinct. I'm not even going to bother fighting it, not worth my time."

"Well, which state is lucky enough to get you this time?" Leena tried to mask her sadness with annoyance.

"Still Michigan."

"No?" her tone grew irritable.

"Oh yeah, I'm being moved to CPD!" Samuel couldn't help but smile.

"What in the hell did I do to deserve this much hatred from the universe!" Leena barked, throwing her fist into the wall. "Is it your goal to piss me off?"

Before Samuel had the chance to get a word in, a group of newbie bluecoats charged through the door. Hands on their weapon, they were ready to protect the precinct. Growing defensive, Leena allowed the anger to consume her. Fangs growing and eyes fixed, ready to defend herself.

"Leena! Enough!" Samuel was quick to recognize Leena's change. Throwing himself between her and the newbies. He pushed her against the wall with a single hand, while using the other to wave the officers away.

"Back off!" she growled. "I don't have time to deal with this bullshit!" Ripping his hand away from her body, Leena stormed out of the conference room. Riding the elevator to ground level, she abandoned Samuel, leaving him to deal with the new officers.

12

Leaving the precinct, the cold pressed against Samuel's skin. Shivering, he ran his hands up and down his arms, a failed attempt to keep warm. Bracing himself against the harsh November winds, he looked around for Leena. Noticing her familiar jacket, Samuel witnessed Leena pressed up against the brick wall.

"What do you want?" she pushed herself away from the wall. "I am not in the mood right now."

"Look, I didn't request to go to Coleman. When you stormed out of the precinct, I called James. Figured he could tell me what the hell is going on with you."

"And?"

"Well, for one I guess I need to apologize. I wasn't aware of what you were going through. Do you have a place to go during the full moon?" Samuel brushed her hair from her eyes.

"I'm staying at Eternal Night, with Raphael," Leena gently pushed his hand away. "He has a basement equipped with chains."

"Kinky," Samuel laughed, harder than he probably should have. "I wonder what else he uses those for." Samuel's comment forced a daggered glance from Leena. Knowing he allowed foolish words to escape his lips, he took a step back.

"We only have a few days before the full moon. I am dealing with so much chaos because of Philip. If I am being honest, I have no idea how the hell I am going to handle it," Leena ran a shaking hand through her hair.

With the wind picking up, they were forced to step back into the precinct. Looking out the windows, they watched cars pass and couples walk down the street hand in hand. Before long, snow began to fall, blanketing the Earth. The sunlight beamed off of the beautiful, icicle decorated, leafless trees. Their gaze was broken as Leena's phone rang, blaring music from her pocket.

"Hi, Mark!" Leena stepped away from Samuel.

"How are you feeling?"

"Could be better, I'm at the Claresville Police Station with Samuel. Had to answer a few questions."

"Samuel! Wait, he's back?" his voice forcing her to pull the phone away. "When did that happen?"

"I don't know," she spoke softly.

After a few moments of chatter and a small argument over Samuel, Leena swiped her finger across the screen, hanging up on Mark during his rant. Growing tired of the dull, dank building, Leena zipped her jacket, braced herself for the reckless winds and stepped outside. The wind whipped her hair around, viciously. Snow struck her skin, feeling as if tiny, frozen needles were attempting to pierce her body. By now, inches upon inches of snow had covered the ground and any other stationary object.

Blizzards such as these would often frequent Claresville, with a small portion of the storms rarely hitting Coleman. When it came to weather, it felt to Coleman's natives that they possibly lived under a dome. Aside from the nice, warm summer days, every other form of weather, from rain to snow, seemed to split around the town. Coleman was seldom hit by harsh weather, but when it was, they sure got it and it would hit, violently. For the most part the Coleman residents felt grateful for the lack of insane weather.

Leena stood in the cold, so focused that she was unable to shiver. Wishing for the day to come to an end, she ducked to the side of the building, escaping the brutal winds. Listening to the sounds of cars and slush on the road, she would hear the occasional horn of a pissed off driver. Inhaling deeply, she felt the cold freeze her nasal cavity and a familiar scent began to creep up on her.

"Samuel, if you're going to be working with the CPD there are a few things you need to know."

"Such as?" he spoke, coming around the corner. "Is my cologne really that strong?"

"Wasn't the cologne that gave you away. When people get excited, they put off a certain smell. Just like fear smells different than sadness."

"Should've known that," Samuel stood closer to Leena, further protecting her from the cold.

"Captain Sommers has no problem with the supernatural. She can be a bitch, it's definitely her way or the highway. We've learned how to keep some things out of her knowledge."

"Like?"

"Well, this case for example. I'm not letting her know anything about Philip. When we keep things from her, it's only to protect her. Pisses her off sometimes."

"Who hides things from her?" Samuel was now chilled to the bone. Shaking vigorously like a washing machine on super spin cycle. "Just you, James, Mark and Matt?"

"Mostly, yeah. We're really the only ones who deal with the over-the-top cases."

With no signs of the wind or snow dying down, Leena remembered the coffee house just next door. Grabbing Samuel by the sleeve, she pulled him behind her, dragging him through the café doors. Heat struck their bodies, and the smell of freshly ground coffee filled their noses. Approaching the counter, they saw employees scampering from one side to the other. Clicking the power buttons on the coffee grinders and throwing syrup into the dispensers, the workers were getting ready for the lunch time rush. Looking up to the order board, Leena saw the hand on the old, wood carved, castle designed cuckoo clock strike two, letting out two long chimes.

"Do you offer Dr. Plasma, Type-A?" Leena searched the boards coming up empty handed.

"No ma'am, sorry," the young man behind the counter looked her in the yes. Recognizing what Leena was, he began to lift a corner of his lip, exposing a fang. "Just your typical coffee, tea and basic high school, white girl Starbucks beverages," the young vampire couldn't have been any less excited about his place of employment.

Looking the newborn vampire deep in the eyes, Leena allowed a small chuckle to escape her lips. Knowing it must be hard for a vampire to work in a place that is against supernatural beings, she ordered two regular coffees and gave a quick smile to the unhappy vampire behind the register. As she grabbed the drinks from his hands, she slid him a rather large tip. With supernatural beings having been out of the shadows for decades, Leena was always baffled how a town could shun a whole race. If one vampire did something wrong, then the whole species as a whole is evil. The one thing the Claresville townsfolk were very well known for was chasing unwanted supernatural out of their town.

After a few caffeinated refills and a lengthy conversation about Philip, they left the table, leaving the cups at the counter. The new vampire smiled, waved them out the door and braced himself for the rush of humans to flood through the doors for their afternoon coffee. She cracked another smile in return, not a full one, just enough to alert him that it will all be okay. Spinning back towards Samuel, a horde of humans all on their phones, oblivious to their surroundings, practically plowed over both Leena and Samuel. Irritated, he threw a few choice words out at the people who continued to ignore his presence.

Finding themselves once again standing in the cold, she unlocked her phone and dialed the cab company. Finishing her call, Leena looked over to her slow pacing friend. Slowly creeping up on him, she placed a light hand on his shoulder.

"Your demeanor changed rather quickly," she spun him to face her. "What are you thinking about?"

"The move to the Coleman department, everything you told me about Philip and I'm not sure why, but I'm thinking about that poor kid at the Claresville Café."

"Why?" she raised a brow. Samuel wasn't normally one to show concern for anyone. Maybe Leena, but even that was touch and go at times, depending on her attitude.

"Just seems wrong that someone so young had their life taken from them and is now forced to work in a town where he is hated!" he threw his hand in the air, pointing to the building that was now packed with people, forcing a line into the cold. "Humans really will do anything for stupid, caramel flavored beverages."

"How can you be so sure he wasn't one of those new age, stereotypical, vampire book loving kids who wanted to be a vampire?"

"You of all people should know the look of someone who was forced into the immortal, bloodlust way of life, Leena!" Samuel grew angered, his sentence full of carefully controlled rage.

Leena was cautious to avoid angering him any further. His fiery, blackout rage was something even vampires feared. Phoenixes may not spontaneously burst into flames at any given time, but their temper, that was in many opinions quite comparable. Allowing Samuel a moment to breathe, she proceeded to shoot a quick text to James, letting him know her estimated time of arrival. Waiting for him to break the silence, Leena paced around, kicking up the snow and slush. She appeared as if she were a child playing in the snow for the first time.

The cabs headlights broke into view, fighting to light the way to the café. With the cabbie sliding to a stop, Leena was forced to jump back to avoid becoming a human slushie. Samuel, now calmed from his earlier rant, found himself laughing. A laugh that Leena was unfamiliar with, a true laugh, not a fake, I'm really dying on the inside laugh. It was times like this that Leena knew no matter how supernatural you really were, you always had a sliver of humanity left inside.

Climbing into the cab, Leena flashed her badge to the driver. Without hesitation, he began the long, boring trip to the Coleman Police Department. Both Leena and Samuel looked out the windows, snow flew by, it looked to them as if they were in a spaceship that just reached warp speed. Considering the ride to be a mini vacation, they slouched in their seats, closing their eyes for a moment of silence and relaxation.

13

Upon arrival at the Coleman Police Department, the cabbie, with as much caution as he could muster, pulled the car to the curb. Tapping his knuckles on the protective glass that guarded him from any crazed or drunken passengers, he startled both Leena and Samuel back to reality. Stretching as best they could, Samuel reached into his back pocket, plucked his wallet from his properly pressed khakis, and browsed through, looking for exact change. Sliding the cash through the small slit just above the center console, the driver slowly grabbed the money, counted twice, and gave a quick thumbs up. Clicking the button to unlock the doors, they took a moment to enjoy the silence and stepped out. Claresville may be a boring old town, but they are known for great crime, it's not unusual for the cab drivers to have complete control over the vehicle. Hell, even the windows are controlled by the one behind the wheel.

Leaving them to stand in the cold, they looked up to the precinct, took a larger than necessary deep breath and made way to the clean Coleman building. If Coleman in general was great at one thing, it was keeping buildings, roads, and parks remarkably clean. Swiping her card through the slot, the intercom chimed, and light blinked green. Throwing the door open, Leena stepped to the side allowing Samuel first entrance into the building. She had a thing about being in front of people while entering any building, possibly due to lack of ability to protect yourself.

Approaching the front desk, Leena was quick to notice the lack of the poor officer that got stuck with desk duty. Assuming the officer was grabbing a coffee, she led Samuel through the double doors. With two elevators on each side, Leena quickly hit the closest button, leaving them to await the arrival of their ride.

A long wait had Leena wondering if the elevators were even in operation. After moments of waiting, the bell let out an annoying ding as the doors slid apart. Once again forcing Samuel to take the first step, she pressed the button with a large three on it. The metallic doors slid shut, soft music began to play, and they felt the jerk of the elevator as it began to rise.

"So, are you excited to deal with whatever is behind those doors when they open?" Samuel leaned over, giving her a shoulder bump.

"Excited? No. Ready? I guess."

"I'm right here," Samuel reached for her hand. "Just squeeze my hand if you feel angered."

His gesture was shot down as Leena wrenched her hand away. She wasn't one to accept help, she was still upset that she needed to stay with Raphael, however she wasn't going to complain about any sex that happened to take place. The place may have felt like a dungeon, but at least there was a little release. Crossing her arms, she stepped to the side, staying away from Samuel as best she could.

Another lurch of the elevator indicated that they had arrived. Once again playing that waiting game, Leena stood impatiently, hoping for the doors to soon open. With a loud creak, the doors opened, revealing James, Matt and even Mark, all arms crossed. She knew that each expression was filled with anger, even a little confusion as their minds realized Samuel was present as well. Stepping from the elevator, Leena's head was filled with gossip as her ears tuned in on her coworkers whispering behind her back.

Clenching her hands into tight fists, she made her way to her desk.

"You've got about a day and a half of mail sitting on your desk," Mark spoke, his voice irritated. "Wondering if you were ever going to come back!"

"Seriously! I wasn't even gone for a whole day! I'm not sure what the hell all your problems are, but if you have something to say, say it!" Leena barked, slamming her fists on the table with great enough force to crack the wood.

Jerking her away from the table, Samuel calmly walked her to the coffee room. Holding her in place against the wall, he forced her to take a breath. Her eyes seemed to darken; it was almost as if Leena was letting go of her humanity. This close to a full moon, Samuel knew he needed to keep her as calm as possible. Placing her in a chair, he rushed to the fridge, grabbed a flask of Dr. Plasma, and hurried back to her side.

"Leena, do you think it's right for you to be in such a confined and stress inducing place?"

"What are you trying to say?" she glared at him harshly. He knew her well enough that even her trying to strike fear into him wasn't going to work.

"All I'm trying to say is that maybe you should leave this place for a few days."

"I'll be fine! I'm just irritated that all this work falls on me. Is everyone here incapable of working on a case without me?"

"No, no they aren't. When you don't check in, we all get worried," a familiar voice entered the room. "They care for you, that's all."

Spinning in her chair, Leena witnessed Captain Sommers leaning against the wall. Wondering how long she had been standing there, her eyes widened. Staying calm so as to not alert the captain to anything out of the ordinary, Leena left the chair, gave a quick nod to Samuel, and made her way back to her desk. Mark had disappeared, but James and Matt were still there, gazing at her. Carefully sitting down, Leena gave a small, crooked mouth smile, hoping that they would forgive her outburst.

Slouching in her chair, her friends remained seated across from her. Thumbing through her mail, she saw a black envelope, no return address, no markings, just her name and the address of the precinct. Opening the letter, Leena leaned forward, elbows on the desk and paper placed just inches from her eyes. Silently mouthing the words to herself, she was brought to a quick halt, clenched her jaw, and crushed the paper between her hands.

"Son of a bitch," she tried to keep her whisper to herself. "What the hell am I going to do!"

"What?" both James and Matt leaned closer.

"That jackass is blackmailing me!"

Tilting their heads in confusion, they went to grab the paper. Unwilling to pull them into this drama, she grabbed the paper, put it in her drawer and locked the desk. Perfect timing as Captain Sommers was once again making her way in Leena's direction. Looking away, she faked being busy. Having no interest in Leena or her problems, she walked by her boots echoing in the eerily quiet room.

"So, where is the information you received from Megan Thorne?" Leena looked directly at James.

"Right. We were in the process of putting the Hayes case to rest, when she contacted us, requesting a meeting. When we met, she said that she wanted to clear the air with you. As you were unavailable, she was hoping to leave a message."

"Which was?"

"To tell you that she has remembered a bit more about that day," he spoke. "Are you really going to hide this blackmail letter from us?" James added, tapping a finger to the desk.

"You bet," Leena spoke, quickly dialing the phone.

Concealing their irritation towards Leena, they left the table, leaving Leena to her thoughts. Waiting impatiently for the continuous ringing to be interrupted by

Megan's voice, she repeatedly clicked her pen. Close to giving up, Leena was welcomed by an annoying, almost nasally voice.

"Hello?" Megan spoke. "Terribly sorry, I'm dealing with a cold."

"Megan?" Leena spoke, ignoring the obviously faked ailment. "This is Detective Rose, CPD, you had left a message with my partner."

"Yes, good afternoon," Megan's voice was suddenly and shockingly less nasally, but just as annoying.

Ignoring her attempt to be friendly, Leena was quick to interrupt. "What time are you available to come down to the station?" she spoke, reaching for her pad of rainbow sticky notes.

"I will be there within the hour," Megan spoke softly.

"Make it thirty minutes!" Leena gave her no time to respond, hanging up the phone. She leaned back in her chair, ran a hand through her long, wavy, knotted up brown hair. She ignored the fact that she looked like an obvious mess.

With time to kill, Leena made way for the breakroom where James sat, alone. Rummaging through the fridge, she looked for any type of Dr. Plasma. A failed attempt as usual, she found herself settling for coffee, shitty coffee. When anyone took the slightest sip of this caffeinated crap, they always walked away with grit in their teeth. With so much of the vampire race depending on the synthetic form of blood, one would think that your establishments would furnish it a bit more often.

Falling into the chair, she kicked her feet up on the table, looked James in the eyes and with a great deal of courage, sipped her drink. Laughing, James slid over a handful of wannabe sugar packets. Placing his cup in the sink, he once again sat next to his partner.

"Your kind will always confuse me," James looked her in the eyes.

"How so?"

"You're a hybrid, which means you no longer have a complete blood dependency, yet you prefer to drink Dr. Plasma. Why?"

"James, when you've lived off of something for so long, it just becomes the normal for you. I can easily go without it, but I have learned that it helps to keep my anger induced bloodlust at bay," Leena took another disgusting sip of coffee. "If I am feeling off in any way, I'll crack open a flask of Dr. Plasma and be on my way."

"Well you must always be on edge," he laughed, harder than he should've.

"I'm a vampire and a werewolf all rolled into one! I have a full moon making me irritated and spiteful 24/7! I'm always hungry because of it! You'd be living off of Dr. Plasma as well if you had to deal with this bullshit! So yes, James, I am on edge, thank you!"

Still laughing, he left the breakroom to meet with Matt. If there was one thing on this planet that Leena found happiness in, it was the love between James and Matt. Vexatious as it was at times, she was happy for James and his engagement. With just minutes to spare, Leena forced herself back to her desk, preparing for her questioning with Megan. Cleaning her desk, she opened the drawer where her attention was quickly drawn to the black envelope.

"Detective?" Captain Sommers ripped Leena's attention away from her desk. "Before your interrogation with Miss Thorne, I'd like to ask you something, if I may?"

"By all means," Leena pointed to the seat across her desk.

"Do I need to worry about Detective Blackhorn?"

"No," Leena cocked her head to one side. "If you're asking if he is human? The answer is also no. He is a Phoenix. Long story short, he is immortal, really has no way of dying, that we know of. When a phoenix is born, their mother, soon after the birth is engulfed in flames. They leave their ashes for their son to be buried in and reborn if for any reason a phoenix is killed before the age of thirty. I don't have time to explain it, just know he is damn good at what he does."

"What if he has his head lopped off?" Captain Sommers was now filled with curiosity.

"Really?" Leena glared at her annoyingly. "We don't have time for this, I don't have time for this!"

Looking away from the captain, she shook her head. She wasn't the encyclopedia of monsters. Why everyone thought she was, was a mystery. If anyone could answer those questions, it'd be Mark. Somehow, witches are scary well versed in all things mythological and supernatural. Looking at her computer clock, Leena saw it strike a new hour, just as Megan was walking through the doors.

"Afternoon Miss Thorne," Leena extended a hand, offering a hearty handshake.

"Megan, please?" she asked, returning the gesture.

"I hear you have more information regarding the death of Austin Hayes. Is this correct?" Leena clicked her pen.

"Not regarding the death, it is however regarded to who I think is at fault."

With great interest, Leena was quick to sit straight in her chair, pen to paper. Being sure to have all her attention on Megan, Leena tuned out the usual office noises. Knowing what was sitting in her desk, she was hoping for any link to the letter.

"Go on."

"In my opinion, I feel that it was the bimbo he was cheating on me with."

"You mean the one that you tossed out? The one you fought with as neighbors watched?" Leena was quick to grow irritable.

"Yes," Megan's tone changed as she realized her story might not match up.

"So, please explain to me how that is possible?"

"I'm not quite sure, I feel like after I left, she went back upstairs to take her anger out on him."

"Megan, I'm not a goddamn idiot! People watched her leave! Do you have anything important to tell me?" Leena used all the control she had not to throw the woman across the room.

Leaning towards Leena, Megan took the pen from her hand and looked her deep in the eyes. With an eerie smile, she looked around the room, noticing that for a Tuesday afternoon, it was rather quiet. Not even a cricket was chirping from a dark corner. They sat in silence for a moment, Leena was already thinking of ways to defend herself. She still had an odd feeling about Megan. Breaking the silence, she continued to look at Leena, she looked as though she lost all control of her thoughts, like her words and actions were controlled by another source.

"You know the answer. It shouldn't take you that long to figure this out," Megan was now dead eyed, zombie like. It was as if someone else was speaking for her.

"What?" Leena whispered; her brow furrowed. Growing tired, she leaned back in her chair, wood creaking and howling with age.

She was unable to get further information out of Megan, who was now bidding her a farewell. Leena sat back in the chair, threw her pen across the room, and watched as Megan entered the elevator. She was pissed, no information was given, and Leena had no time to waste on people lying to her. Rubbing her eyes, she plucked the letter from her drawer, gently placing it on her desk. Before she had a chance to reread the note, her phone buzzed across the desk.

"What do you want?" her question was more anger filled than anything else.

"It's her, she did it! She killed Austin!" Mark's voice was loud enough, that through the phone he allowed anyone that passed by the chance to hear him.

"What the hell are you talking about!"

"Megan, it was Megan! She killed Austin; it all makes sense now!"

Leena, dropped her phone on the desk, ignoring the shouting that was irrupting from her phone speakers. Standing up, she kicked the chair away, forcing it to speed across the office. Feeling as though she was unable to move, Leena stood in place, her hands grew clammy and a bead of sweat ran from her brow, down her pale skin.

Knowing all too well that Megan was long gone; she didn't let that get her down. Finding herself jumping over desks, Leena stood at the elevator, smashing the down button, hoping that would hurry her ride. Giving up on the slower than normal elevator, she threw open the doors and sped down the stairs, skipping a staircase occasionally. Bursting through the doors which led to the main floor, Leena looked around for any sign of Megan, no familiar faces, no recognizable scents. She disappeared and Leena was left empty handed.

14

A few days had come and gone, not a single trace of Philip or Megan emerged. Mark had decided to spend a few days with Leena at Eternal Night, resulting in a few failed attempts of the occasional locator spell. With the morning light pouring in from the windows, both Leena and Mark were ripped from their deep slumbers. Stretching her muscles, she rolled off the bed, landing hard on the floor. Laughing, Mark rolled across the carpet, tapped Leena on the shoulder, making sure she was okay. Glancing at the calendar that was carefully hung above Raphael's desk, Leena was quick to notice the date.

"Shit!" she sprung to her feet. "You can't be here!"

Tilting his head to the side, Mark rubbed the sleep from his radiant, icy blue eyes. Standing up, he did a full body stretch, which forced him to shake. We all know that stretch you do in bed that has your legs shaking like a dog getting its belly scratched. Fixing his clothes, he walked over to the calendar, placed his finger on the specifically marked date, let out a single chuckle and made way for the bathroom.

"You laugh, but you have no idea what is going to happen today, Mark!" Leena found herself yelling and slamming a fist against the door.

"Ocupado!" he laughed.

"Mark, this isn't something to laugh about. Look what happened to you a few days ago, that was just days before a full moon."

"And you survived it then, you'll survive it now."

"How?" Leena spoke, worried. She tried to hide how she was feeling, but Mark knew better.

Hearing the faucet run, Leena opened the door, looked him in the eyes, awaiting a response. Exiting the bathroom, Leena gave him the look of, are you going to flush or not. Ignoring her glance, he flicked a hand in the air, causing the toilet handle to move, flushing itself. Making their way down the stairs, the smell of freshly brewed coffee and fresh baked, blueberry scones filled their noses.

"Morning love," Raphael smiled. "Morning, Mark," his smile began to fade away.

"Morning," they spoke in unison, inhaling the intoxicating aroma.

"What did I do to be pampered this morning?" Mark laughed, snapping a finger, forcing a scone to fly from the counter to his hand.

Ignoring Mark, he made his way towards Leena, extended his arms for a morning embrace, and leaned in for a kiss. Placing a hand on his mouth, she slowly shoved him away. Brushing off Leena's rejection, he turned to the bar, poured a larger than normal cup of coffee and left for the office.

"Little harsh, don't you think?" Mark looked to Leena. "We all know you two are a "thing", no need to hide it."

"Shut up, jackass!" Leena continued to enjoy her morning drink.

"Is it Samuel?" Mark sat himself next to her, silence filled the room. "It is, isn't it?"

"It's not that easy, Mark."

"Of course it is. If you want Samuel, choose him, if not, choose Raphael," he gave her a pat on the shoulder, her silence continued. "Unless you want them both?" his tone grew curious.

Leena looked off into the distance, ignoring Mark. Finishing their breakfast, they gathered their belongings and made way to Leena's borrowed car, which was finally back from the Claresville Auto Shop. Clicking the start button on her key fob, the car roared to life.

"Three days of this Megan bullshit! Where the hell could she have gone?"

"Forget that. How have we not heard anything from Philip? He sends you a blackmail letter and then disappears."

"Mark, don't make me regret reading you that note!" Leena glared over the roof.

"What did it say again? I still don't understand why Philip would compel Megan to act like a fool, only to tell you vague, already known information about Austin's death."

"If you don't speak the truth and comply with my demands, I will kill everyone close to you, humiliate you. Last chance, Leena. The only question you need to ask yourself is whether or not you can handle the task at hand?" Leena spoke quietly.

Both Leena and Mark fell into the car and sat for a moment of silence. The heat of their bodies forced the windows to fog over. Looking each other deep in the eyes, Leena threw the car into reverse. Speeding away from the building, she forced the car into the annoyingly condensed Coleman traffic. Fighting to get from lane to lane, Leena would occasionally punch the horn, scaring the oblivious drivers who were unwilling to follow the simplest of traffic rules. Mark and Leena were beginning to grow increasingly irritated. With cars using various off ramps, the traffic was finally bearable. Keeping each other calm, with the sporadic rant due to the idiocy of younger drivers, they were interrupted by Leena's phone ringing from within the car speakers.

"Detective! We have a little surprise for you. Someone is in our custody," James echoed through the phone.

"Philip?" Leena found herself pressing the volume up button on her steering wheel in an attempt to not miss a word.

"Megan, actually," she could hear how prideful James was. "She was found downtown, sitting under the bridge in Coleman Park, almost zombie like."

"And?" Leena tried to coax more out of James.

"That's it, I mean we cuffed her, brought her here and she has been sitting in a cell for about an hour now."

"Why the hell am I only just now getting a call?" Leena barked at her radio.

"Can't very well say anything when Captain Sommers is roaming the office, can I?" he barked back. "You don't want her to know anything, so we, Matt and I, have to be cautious. In my opinion it would be easier for her to know, but who am I to judge."

"Exactly, not you!" Leena hung up the phone. "Jackass," she added in a whisper.

Ignoring Mark's attempt to begin another conversation, Leena jerked the wheel to the right, taking a tight turn towards the precinct. Causing her vehicle to fishtail, she gathered control of the car, fixed her eyes on the snow-covered road, and ignored Marks annoyed scoff. A few cars parked on the side of the road, four-ways flashing, indicating caution to other drivers. The snow was heavy, more so than usual. With an awkward, silent drive, Mark found himself playing mindless games on his phone, knowing all too well that Leena had no desire to speak.

15

Awaiting the arrival of Leena, James pulled Megan from the cell, cautiously walked her to the interrogation room where he prepared her for questioning. Locking Megan in place, her wrists were held down by handcuffs linked to the table. Seating himself across from her, he kicked his feet up on the table, looked her in the eyes and winked in a manner of, you've been caught, good luck getting away this time. Keeping his eyes on Megan, she proceeded to occupy the silence with an eerie whistle.

"Miss Thorne?" James, growing irritable, forced the whistle to stop.

Looking James deep in the eyes, she made a feeble attempt to lunge towards James. Jumping with a hint of fear, he used all the power he could to hide any fear he may be showing. Placing his feet firmly on the floor, he glared at Megan, clenched a fist, holding back the urge to threaten her. Probably in his best interest. As a ghostly smile grew on Megan's face, James felt himself growing warmer and warmer. Tugging on his tie, he loosened the knot, fanning himself with a pad of paper to cool off. Megan, her smile now ear to ear was laughing, quietly to herself.

Continuing to fan his chest and neck, he was quick to notice that Megan was leaning back in her chair comfortably. Growing confused, he sat back in the chair, sipped water, and undid the top button to his shirt. Letting out an unearthly laugh, Megan's eyes almost seemed to blacken. She clenched her fists, laughed harder and shook her head in a maddening fashion. Stepping away from the crazed woman, he watched as she threw her hands open. Flames began to engulf Megan, her hair, which was soon replaced by an inferno was the first to go. Spitting embers throughout the room.

Before the flames could grow out of control, James was violently pushed to the side as Leena barreled through the doors. Grabbing the glass on the table, Leena threw the water in Megan's face, causing her hot head to die out. Coughing, Megan continued to find herself doused in water, choking for air. The woman truly resembled a hissing, freshly extinguished campfire. Feeling like it was time to take a little break, Leena set another chair at the table. Escorting James out the door, she soon returned to Mark, who was mumbling a few words, prohibiting Megan from being able to set herself ablaze. Setting herself next to her friend, she was sure to keep focus on Megan.

"We meet again, Miss Thorne!" Leena took a deep breath, tapping her pen on the table.

Megan continued to sit in silence, grinning at both Leena and Mark. Knowing she couldn't do them any physical harm with Mark quietly preventing her fiery explosions, Leena flipped open her pad of paper. Placing the tip of the pen to the paper, she made a small bullet point indicating where her first note will go.

"Megan, I'm going to cut to the chase! What are you?"

"Kitsune, level nine, that's the tattoo behind your ear," Mark didn't allow Megan to answer, at this point he wasn't even willing to let her breathe.

"A what?" confusion struck Leena.

"Kitsune. Someone cursed with the spirit of the fire fox. Well to them it's a blessing. Me, I'd consider that a curse. The first case of Kitsune was discovered in Japan, long ago, roughly the 19th century. Since then, they have found not only a fire fox, but various other fox spirits as well. Once again, thank you grimoires!" Mark threw out the knowledge with ease, still counteracting Megan, and her uncontrollable blaze.

Leena sat in silence, confusion, rage, and annoyance filled her thoughts. Stepping out of the room, she left Mark with Megan. Knowing he could handle himself; she didn't worry. The ding of the elevator across the way forced Leena to jump, afraid that Captain Sommers was going to step through the doors, she rushed over only to witness Samuel jumping from the metallic room. Slapping the back of his head, she threw an arm around his neck, forcing him to follow. Tripping over his feet, he struggled to keep balance as Leena's unforgiving grip felt like it was soon going to rip his head from his shoulders. Pulling away from Leena, he took a step back, looked her in the eyes, head slightly tilted to the side. She waved a hand; he didn't need words for Samuel to know he must follow.

"Leena, dammit! What is going on?" he barked, alerting his presence to everyone in the office, including James.

"We have no time to chat. Right now, Captain Sommers is out, and I need to get every answer I can before she gets back. We have a damned Kitsune in the interrogation room!"

"A What?"

"Exactly, Mark can explain it. She either is or was working with Philip, I'm assuming."

"Another quick, yet slightly unrelated question. Why did you pounce at me in the elevator?"

"Thought you were the captain."

"Yeah, where is she anyway?"

"Last day before vacation, running some errands for the office. That's not what is important!" Leena's voice was filled with a low growl.

"Full moon getting the best of you?"

Leena ignored Samuel and his snide remark, reached for the handle of the door, allowing him to enter first. Looking the woman up and down, Samuel was forced to fan himself, keeping himself cool. She may not have set the room ablaze, but it was still warmer than necessary.

Smiling back at him, Megan gave him a quick wink and a small, choked laugh.

"The hell are you laughing at?" Leena was once again throwing water in Megan's face.

"Nothing, I just know you can't hold me here for long. I'm close with the Chief of Police!"

"I'm glad to hear the Chief of Police is such a close personal friend of yours, at least you know someone who can post your bail." Leena laughed, pointing to Mark indicting that he needs to make the spell a little stronger.

Binding Megan, he felt safe enough to break his concentration and focus on the main point at hand, Megan being the kitsune and their problem all along. Leaving her in the cold, unreasonably damp room, the three of them stood outside the door. It seemed as though everyone was either hard at work, which was unlikely, or they all new better than to interrupt Leena and the gang. Standing in silence, Leena, Mark, and Samuel found themselves pacing around, subconsciously following one another. Periodically looking into the interrogation room, they would slow down just enough to make sure Megan was still under control.

"I don't feel like this is all over, Leena," Mark broke the eerie silence.

"How so?"

"It's one of those feelings, the ones I usually get when I feel like something is off," he winked.

Acknowledging his action, Leena broke from the group, entered the room, and closed the door behind her. Hesitant to approach Megan, she pulled the chair away a few feet and sat herself close to the door, ready for a quick getaway. Eyeing the newly discovered Kitsune, Leena made a quick choice to once again douse Megan in cold water.

"It really doesn't matter how soaked I am, I'll get out today. I'm not worried."

"Pretty cocky for someone who can quite literally be placed at a murder. You know Austin Hayes, don't you?" Leena scribbled a few notes in her book.

"I'll hand it to you, Leena. You're not as dim as you look!"

"So, why do it? Why kill him?"

"As much as I loved him, do you really think I would kill Austin? Willingly that is?" Megan was once again choked up, but not due to the water. Her words now felt controlled by her, instead of an unknown source

Watching a single drop of water roll from the corner of her eye, down her cheek, Leena found herself in a deep thought. "If someone killed in a manner such as this, why would they feel any kind of remorse? There are still so many questions." Leena allowed herself to breathe, relax her muscles and focus on Megan. Close to a breakdown, she struggled to wipe the tear from her face.

"Here," Leena placed a tissue in her hand. "Don't try anything!"

Losing her grip, Megan lost it, streams of tears now rolling down her face. Calling out for Austin, she would pause to recall a memory. Confusion gripped Leena, she was lost, there was nothing that could explain her breakdown.

"Megan? When they found you, you were under the park bridge. Do you remember how you got there?"

"No," she tried to hold back tears, it just resulted in crying induced hiccups. "Everything from Austin's death to now feels like a blur. I can recall extraordinarily little."

Realizing her attitude came from a place of sorrow, bewilderment and anger, Leena unlocked Megan's cuffs. Rubbing her wrists, the room was suddenly filled with a bang, as Mark and Samuel were barreling through the door. Flicking his wrist, Mark threw Megan against the back all. This time using some unseen force to suffocate the life from Megan's body. Quickly grabbing another set of cuffs, Samuel made his way to assist Mark.

The struggle in the room grew quite excessive for Leena. Finding herself out of control, she slammed her hand against the table. Leaving a sizeable hole in the metal,

Leena threw them out of the way, picked Megan up off the ground and set her in the corner. The moon was quickly taking control and it wasn't even night. Standing up, both Mark and Samuel fixed their clothing, fixed their hair, and took a few steps back. Fear was in their eyes as Leena was not in a normal state of mind. Her fangs grew, eyes darkened, and her posture was less than satisfactory. At this point, she was almost a whole new person.

"Don't touch her!" Leena barked, keeping Megan in a corner.

"Leena! She is uncontrollable, she can't be let loose, not after what she did!" both Samuel and Mark tried to reason with her.

"I don't think it was all her. Her actions, but not her plan," Leena was retracting her fangs, looking somewhat normal again.

"What the hell are you talking about?" Samuel's confusion had him pissed off.

"I don't remember doing anything," Megan chimed in.

"Bitch! I don't want to hear from you!" Mark was again making his presence known.

Grabbing the collar of his neatly pressed button-down shirt, she tossed him outside the room. Peering through the window, Mark resembled a puppy being home alone for the first time. Occasionally pressing himself against the door, it all led to failed attempts at eavesdropping.

"Fine! Explain!" Samuel leaned himself against the furthest wall, being careful to avoid getting close.

"Our day was like any other. We went to the gym; Austin did his usual muscle growing routine and I went for a run. Everything was fine until we reached the apartment. I remember seeing someone we usually workout with. Kristee, Kristee Jane was her name, she lived one floor above us. I was filled with hate and for some reason I knew Austin was cheating on me, with her. I haven't felt this normal in a while, dumping the water on me snapped me out of whatever fog I was in."

"Megan, did you talk to anyone out of the ordinary at the gym?" Samuel interjected.

"I'm a talkative chick, I make friends quite easily."

"Samuel?" Leena looked to him. "Go get Mark!"

As he made his way to grab Mark from the dimly lit hallway, Leena put the room back in order. Allowing Megan to actually enjoy the water, she placed the chairs around the table. Awaiting the arrival of Mark, she tucked away her pen and paper, putting the energy of the room at ease.

"What? Now my attendance is necessary?" Mark snapped at Leena.

"Do you have your stuff with you?"

"Stuff? Oh that, yeah. Why?" Mark was still angered, and rightfully so.

"Grab it, I think we need a reading," Leena winked, tilting her head to Megan.

Happy that it was his time to shine, he grabbed his bag from the hallway. Rummaging through the bag, it looked as if his entire arm disappeared. Both Megan and Samuel looked at him, tilted their heads and watched in awe. Hearing what sounded like things falling over in the bag, Leena laughed, knowing his endless bag spell caused less organization than he thought. Placing another arm in the bag, they heard him fixing the books. His eyes widened as he felt his beloved tarot deck brush his hand. Mark was well versed in reading all forms of tarot cards. They can be used for many things, to glance at a possible future, romance or in the hands of someone as powerful as Mark, they could be used to see into the past.

Placing the cards on the table, he closed his eyes, waved a hand over his cards, and tapped the deck. A fog formed slowly over the cards. As they were lifted from the table, they seemed to shuffle themselves. Separating into small groups of five, they landed softly on the table, forming a pentacle, the sacred five-pointed star. A heartbeat had passed and the cards, all but five, formed a circle around the remaining group. Snapping his fingers, the cards revealed themselves, starting from the top point and continued clockwise. Revealing a reading that left Mark with a dropped jaw and clenched fists.

"So?" Leena looked at the cards, confused. "What do they say?"

"I'd say take a guess, but as my current stance states, I don't think I need to say much. She received The High Priestess, The Magician, Three of Swords, reversed Two of Swords and The Devil. Simply put Priestess is Megan, a powerful woman, The Magician indicated a trickster she has recently met, and the Three of Swords shows us that she was in a sense, stabbed in the back. The remaining cards, Two of Swords shows us that as of current she is lost, confused, and overloaded. Her final card however indicates that she is trapped, not free of her past," Mark read the tarot spread as calmly as he could.

"Philip?" Leena whispered to herself, hoping she kept her voice low enough. She didn't.

"I knew it," Samuel spoke, forming a fist.

16

With hours passing by, Megan was soon freed of her cage. Making a point to keep her safe, Leena ordered a 24-hour watch. Unwilling to deal with Philip any more than she needed to, she found herself reading the blackmail letter she had received. With Mark back at the morgue, Samuel on a coffee run and James checking in on Matt, who was taking the full moon pretty hard, she found herself checking her e-mail and lounging around the office. As Captain Sommers appointed Leena the Head of Office for the duration of her vacation, Leena was finding herself busier than normal. Looking at Austin's case, she kept strict focus hoping to find something that would lead to Philip's whereabouts.

Forcing someone to kill another really was Philip's way of getting the job done, but using compulsion wasn't his usual go to move. It was more I'm going to threaten your life and your family if you don't do as I say. A semi unsolved murder, a Kitsune, Philip missing, and a blackmail letter made for a tough job. Leena knew that if he wanted to be found, he would be. He'd show himself if the time were necessary. Leaning back in Captain Sommers chair, she kicked her feet up, looked through her mailbox and studied what evidence she could. Enjoying her silence, she was quick to realize that it was still November 23rd, the full moon. Swiping across the name James on her phone, she pressed the speaker button and patiently waited for his louder than normal voice to echo through.

"Roadkill Café, you kill, we grill!" James laughed, possibly harder than he should have.

Leena allowed for a beat of silence to fill the air. "James, you're one of my best friends, you know I care for you dearly, but you don't have a comedic bone in your body. It's worse when you try."

"What can I help you with?" his laugh stopped; his tone softened.

"I don't mean to be a buzz kill," she was quick to add. "What are the chances of Matt and I being locked up together? Maybe we could help each other through the night."

"It's pretty small here. What about Eternal Night? Do you think Raphael would allow that?" James asked cautiously.

"He has some band playing tonight, along with a group meeting. Music, dancing, and drunk idiots. Yeah it could work, no one will hear Matt shifting," Leena spoke as she opened her messenger app to alert Raphael of the evenings plan.

Hanging up the phone, Leena grabbed the letter once again. If you don't comply with my demands and speak the truth. What the hell does that even mean? Leena thought to herself. Leaning back in the chair, she placed the letter over her face. Looking through the letter, she saw a few markings show through as the light beamed onto the page. Slamming forward in the chair, she ripped the paper from her eyes, placed it on the table and grabbed the magnifying glass from Captain Sommers desk. Nothing, she couldn't see anything. Running to the hall, she grabbed an old overhead projector, plugged it in, brushed the dust away and placed the paper on the glass. Clicking the button, the letter was soon projected to the wall. Closing the blinds to the office and locking the door, she studied the paper.

"You have got to be kidding me!" she yelled, hopefully not loud enough to be heard by the office.

Her rant was quickly brought to a halt as a loud banging forced her to freeze in place. Jumping over the desk, she made her way to the door. Peeking through the shades, she saw Samuel, coffee in hand and a big smile on his face.

"Can I come in or do I need a password?" he laughed.

"One moment!"

Letting go of the blinds, they snapped back in place. Samuel could hear Leena playing with the lock, knocking over the chair and slam something against a wall. Growing confused, he took a few steps back, eyed the door, pursed his lips, thinking many thoughts. One more bang and the door slowly began to slide open. Entering the office, Samuel felt almost uneasy, like something was hiding or being hid from him.

"The rest of the team may be dimwitted, but the ruckus clearly means you have something. Spill!"

"Sit and stay quiet!" she barked.

Placing the coffee on the table, he spun a chair around, sat patiently and looked at the mess around him. Slowly walking up to the projector, she clicked the button. Listening to the large object roar to life, the light slowly began to brighten. With the image of the blackmail letter covering most of the wall, Samuel was left sitting, confused. Walking up to the wall, she ran a hand up and down the projected letter.

"Saw this earlier while I was looking at the ceiling," Leena continued to brush her hand against the wall.

"Come again?" he raised a brow, treating her like a fool.

"I was leaning back in the chair, letter over my eyes. When I looked into the light through the letter, I saw words that couldn't be seen by the naked eye," she explained, in return speaking to Samuel like a child.

"Okay?" still confused, but focused, he looked Leena in the eyes.

"Philip thought I was just as dim as the rest of these officers. He hid his plans within the blackmail note! He wrote down everything!" Leena barked.

"What the hell do you mean?"

"He planned on using Megan as a pawn, to gain as much time as he could! He compelled Megan to kill Austin, she, for a while wasn't in control of her own thoughts. I'm sure he has an army now, an army of many different supernatural beings. This is definitely just the beginning," Leena explained. "He kidnaps Luna, almost kills Bella, kills Austin, forces me to deal with inner demons and gets me to deal with a full moon. Smart move Philip, but I am smarter, quicker!" Leena added, hiding the worry as best she could.

"Leena? You can't hide worry from me. So, what's his next move then?"

"To force me to speak the truth, to give him what he wants," she spoke softly, timidly.

"Which is?" Samuel chugged his coffee and without knowledge, he polished of Leena's drink as well.

"I don't know, I don't know what he means by truth. As far as what he wants, that's clear. He wants Coleman, Philip wants to be the new king, he wants me to suffer!"

"I think he'll have to get through Raphael first," he laughed.

Leaving the projected letter on the wall, they sat at the desk, wondering what Philip could do next. Having her own thoughts on what Philip could want truth wise, Leena kept her eyes on the letter. After hours of looking at the letter and other various pieces of evidence, Leena felt herself growing angered, irritable and without reason, very hungry. Coming up seemingly empty handed, Samuel knew it was time he and Leena met with James and Matt at Eternal Night. Flicking off the projector, they gathered their belongings, locked the office behind them, rode the elevator to the ground floor, hopped in the car and made way to the bar.

17

Upon arrival at Eternal Night, Leena looked out the window, witnessing James and Matt making their way in her direction. Pausing just in front of Samuel's vehicle, they waited patiently. Well as patiently as someone transitioning from man to wolf could be. Leena looked to Samuel, placing pressure against her temples in a feeble attempt to rub the pain away. With the night growing closer, they knew it was in their best interest to get inside before the bar opened to the public. Rolling down the window, she heard Matt's alarm go off.

"It's six-o-clock love. We need to get you to safety," James lightly grabbed Matt by the hand, placing the other on his shoulder, guiding him to the door.

Exiting the car, Leena was slightly hunched, the pain of a hybrid transition almost unbearable to her. Placing a gentle hand on her back, Samuel found himself guiding Leena to the doors. A bolt of pain struck her insides, tripping over the curb, Leena met the pavement, face first. Looking up to her friends, a trickle of blood ran from her brow, down her face. Her eyes grew dark, her fangs began to show, and claws stabbed into the cement. Leena's breath grew harsh, her actions led her friends to believe that she wasn't herself.

Gathering around Leena, they heard her breath become uneasy. Eyes now fully dark, a shadow was cast over the group. Spinning around they saw Raphael standing over them, an irritated look on his face. Throwing them out of the way, he looked around, checking for anyone who may be watching in secret. With no one in sight, Raphael tossed Leena over his shoulder, turned, kicked the door open and disappeared into the shadows of Eternal Night. Looking at one another, they all nodded in agreement and followed suit.

As their eyes began to adjust to the abnormally dim room, they witnessed Leena being placed on the bar. Raphael grabbed a cloth, dampened it with cool water and placed it on Leena's forehead. Inhaling deeply, Leena found herself feeling weaker than normal. How could I feel so angered and so strong, then feel so weak? She thought to herself. Her eyes fluttered as she looked in Raphael's eyes, a weak smile formed across her face. Before she knew it, the pain forced her to pass out, lifeless on the bar.

As chimes of the clock brought her back to reality, Leena found herself chained in the basement. A cold, wet floor beneath her feet and the smell of mildew filled her nose. Looking around, she saw Matt was placed in identical chains, only a mere ten feet away from her. His chest was slow to rise and just as slow to fall, he seemed moments from death. Gaining the strength to say his name, she was interrupted as James entered the room, wet rag in hand and a loving expression in his eyes.

"How are you babe?" James spoke, softly placing a kiss on Matt's forehead.

"Been better," Matt smacked his dry lips.

"Drink," James gently placed the glass of water to his lips.

Watching the love between James and Matt caused Leena to smile. Noticing what she was doing, she quickly brought her smile to an immediate halt. Leaning against the pillar, she felt the cold of the chains against her skin. Jumping due to the unnecessary temperature, she felt a hand on her shoulder. It was James, he was trying to keep her calm.

"Leave me, tend to Matt. He's far more important!" she carefully pushed him away.

"Shut up! You're just as important as he is," James gave her a kiss in the forehead and a swift smack to the back of the head. "You're one of my best friends and he is my fiancé, I love you both."

Leena broke, she smiled, and tears welled in her eyes. She wasn't sure if it was just the sheer pain of the full moon or the small amount of love growing for James. Either way she felt the tear to be unnecessary, struggling to bring her hand to her face, she brushed the tear from her eyes. Sipping on the water, she looked around the damp basement, it was inhospitable, lifeless. This resembled a place you would take someone to die, or at least wait for death. Quick to notice that there happened to be more than two large pipes with chains, Leena began to wonder what this was actually used for.

"Raphael! Raphael! Get down here!" Leena allowed a deep throated growl to escape her lips, rattling her chains.

With the full moon rising in the sky, Leena knew it wasn't wise to scream as guests and patrons were soon to arrive. Full moons at Eternal Night were always packed from open to close as young men and women stopped by, hoping to get their jollies off. Humans studied the phases of the moon, placing wedding parties, bachelorette, bachelor parties and other various, sometimes weird gatherings at the bar. It's like people thought that vampires knew how to party better than your average mortal. Truth is, it's not like they partied better, it's just that vampires didn't care. Tonight, however was a business meeting. Men and women from Center Plaza, a large building filled with different businesses, located near the southern part of the state, would come to Eternal Night every so often to discuss future ideas. With the doors slowly opening, Leena could hear the thunderous music flow through the basement. The bass shaking not only the walls, but the chains themselves were forced to rattle, making their own eerie music. Glaring toward the staircase, Leena saw Raphael emerge from the shadows, an annoyed expression stretched across his face.

The music still boisterous, she heard the stomps of people dancing and the high-pitched screech of stool legs against the floorboards. It brought a painful ringing to her ears. Looking Leena in the eyes, Raphael brushed hair from her face, running a soft hand down her cheek.

"Enough!" Leena jerked her head away as best she could. "What's your problem?"

"What was this place?" Leena asked discreetly. "It looks like a goddamned torture chamber."

"Yeah?"

"Yeah what? Do you mean to tell me you still use it as such?" she tried to contain her anger, for Matt's sake.

"No, Leena. It's just a damn basement!"

"Then why do I feel so worried?" she looked around at the blank, wet walls.

"Blame it on the transition. It was once a place he kept humans when it belonged to Mr. Blutsauger. He'd keep people here for his crazy ritualistic meetings."

"Alastair?" Leena whispered. "I never cared for that man."

"It's just a basement now. I don't use it, which if I were you, I'd be pretty grateful for that. Otherwise you'd probably shift out in the open, vulnerable. Now is that something you want with Philip running around?" Raphael spoke, a mix of sass and sarcasm filled his words.

Leena whipped her hands and the chains holding her followed suit. Wrapping themselves around Raphael's neck, Leena jerked the chains to the side, forcing him to the ground. Connecting hard with the cement, a sickening sound filled the room as Raphael's clavicle snapped, protruding from his shoulder. Another jerk of her hands, raising them above her head, she brought him face to face. Looking him in the eyes, he was filled with dread, pain, and confusion. He watched as her eyes again grew dark. Throwing her hands back to the side, she flung Raphael across the basement. More bones cracked; his breath forced from his body as he connected with the wall across the way.

Both James and Matt watched in amazement. Knowing she wasn't herself, he excused himself from the basement, heading back to the party upstairs. Pausing just before the door, he placed his bones back in their correct place, filling the room with more sickening sounds. Slowly healing himself, Raphael was unwilling to scare the paying customers with his bloodied body.

Looking through the small, bar covered windows, both Leena and Matt saw the moon growing, reaching its highest point in the night sky. James continued to dab a damp rag across Matt's forehead, keeping him at peace. With the time growing closer and closer, it seemed as though Leena and Matt would get irritable at the slightest sound. As the light of the moon began to creep through the windows, James knew it was time to leave. His love for Matt was strong, but he knew what was best for them all. Leaving the basement, James looked back to Matt, sadness filled his eyes. Placing a kiss on his palm, he blew on his hand, sending the kiss to Matt. An action they both knew expressed how much they will always love each other.

"If I weren't in so much pain, I'd find that gross," Leena expressed in a weak, disgusted manner.

"You wish you had a love like this," Matt laughed cautiously, unwilling to cause any sudden pain or movements.

Leena was left speechless. The moonlight was again creeping its way toward them. Matt sat on the floor, a single leg extended, trying to keep himself as comfortable as he could. Looking to Leena, Matt was unaware of the light slowly closing in on his leg. Without knowledge, the moonlight touched his leg. Pain shot through his body; he jerked his leg back into the shadows as best he could. The change was close, real close. Both Leena and Matt hoped that the party would last long enough that no one would hear the chaos downstairs.

"Leena?"

"Yes."

"I'm scared," Matt looked her deep in the eyes.

Not wanting to seem weak, she hesitated to respond. "So am I," she spoke softly, keeping him calm.

"Many people think this would be a blessing. Movies show us as awesome fighters, blah, blah, blah. This is a damn curse Leena, a once a month curse! I wouldn't wish this on my worst enemy, and I have a few."

"This is my first time, I don't know what I am in for, but all I can think of is Philip. He has clearly done this before. Is he running around out there causing disarray and death while I sit in here?"

The conversation was brought to a stop as the room was filled with the light of the moon. Dropping to the floor, both Matt and Leena crossed their arms, writhing in pain. Leena's eyes shifted to an eerie yellow color, her fangs growing longer. Throwing her fist to the ground, she left the basement floor with a rather sizeable crack. Dust filled the air with each punch she threw at the cement. Looking to Matt, she saw his eyes had changed, yellow, with a hint of black around the iris. Knowing his pain was greater, she stretched a hand to his, gently placing her palm on his wrist. As heartless as she could be, she knew this couldn't be fun for Matt. He is young, with a curse such as this, it pauses your life. No one should deal with placing their life on hold once a month just to turn into a blood thirsty beast, if anyone knew that it was Leena. Her life felt like it was always paused, she never had a chance to live, even when she was younger, pre vampire.

Leena looked around the room, her claws dug into the floor, her eyes cold and senses heightened beyond anything she has felt. Matt, who was throwing himself against the wall, was dealing with the pain of shifting bones, sprouting fur and claws pushing his nails from his body. The room was filled with screams as Leena made attempt after attempt to break free. Matt, who was now half transitioned, added a mix of howls, barks, and whimpers. Minutes turned to an hour, with both Leena and Matt fully consumed by the power of the full moon. They filled the room with the sound of panting and deep inhales paired with sharp exhaling.

Looking to one another, they had become aware that the chains which held them during the change were no longer keeping them at bay. Running up the stairs, Leena drove her shoulder into the door. Filled with rage and hunger, she pulled her arm back, preparing to throw a fist into the door. Her punch was frozen as Matt wrapped his jaws around her elbow. Ripping her away from the door, he tossed her across the room, leaving her to fall to the floor. Locking their unearthly eyes on each other, Leena jumped to the ceiling, dug her claws in, trying to keep clear of Matt's jaws, she failed. Balancing on his back legs, he pawed at Leena, digging his claws in her back. Blood trickled from her wounds, covering the floor beneath her. Growing angered, Matt, with all the power he could, jumped to Leena, wrapped his fangs around her neck and pulled her to the floor. Shaking Leena like a ragdoll dog toy, he released her, leaving her seemingly lifeless on the floor.

Blood poured from Leena's wounds, no muscle movement. Maybe she's playing opossum? The wolf thought to himself. Matt slowly but carefully walked up to Leena. Nudging Leena with his cold, wet nose, he gently rolled her on her back. Bringing his muzzle close to Leena, he was soon filled with an unbearable, unexplainable pain, unable to move. Leena had dug her hand into Matt's shoulder blade. Blood now ran down her forearm from Matt's wound. Showing him the same pain he caused her, Leena picked him up with one hand, readying the other for a powerful blow. Thrusting her free hand into his chest, she heard the breath forcefully leave his lungs. Thrown from her hands, Matt crashed into the basement wall, dust filled the room, silence consumed the shadows. Standing in spot, weak but triumphant, Leena witnessed that she had successfully knocked the wind out of Matt. Placing her hands to her side, she was overcome with sheer exhaustion, collapsing where she stood, her head bashed against the floor. Leena's sight blurred for a moment, fainting, the basement walls began to fade into darkness.

18

The room was beginning to fill with morning sun. The harsh November cold filled the room through the walls. The Earth was frozen, you couldn't break ground with a shovel. Even the windows couldn't hold back the bitter winds. Ripped from her deep slumber, Leena slightly opened her eyes, the sun felt like it burned her retinas. Squinting to prevent the sun from entering her sight any further, she looked around the room, muscles ached. Groaning at her own pain, she pushed herself against the wall, out of the sun. With the cold of the wall cutting through her, she looked around, trying to find Matt. Her attention was caught by a small movement near the stairs.

"Matt?" Leena spoke softly, her breath still heavy.

"Hey! Welcome back!" both James and Matt spoke in unison.

"How long have we been out?"

"You? The whole weekend. Me, about a day and a half. Always happens after a shift."

Slowly standing up, her legs shook beneath her. Still weak from her full moon shift, she slowly stumbled over to her friends. Collapsing, she found herself leaning against a pillar. Lack of strength was beginning to irritate her. Blowing the bangs from her eyes, she looked up to James who was hovering over her, damp rag, and water in hand.

"Stay calm, there may still be a residual impact from the shift," Leena looked James in the eyes, she heard his words, but saw no movement of his mouth.

"James, how?" she looked lost.

"You took one hell of a beating, Leena. Once all was said and done, I came down to check on Matt. He had changed back and you, you were still out cold. Wounds taking forever to heal," his voice rang in Leena's head once again.

Leaving Leena to chug the glass of water, he made his way back to Matt. Helping his fiancé to button his shirt, he gave him a light pat on the back, kissed his neck and helped him up the stairs. Knowing he was okay in the hands of Samuel, he looked to Leena, smiling. Jumping from the stairs, he took the glass from her hands, set it on the ledge and sat across from her. Looking Leena in the eyes, he saw worry, fear, and exhaustion.

"I sometimes forget faeries have telepathic abilities," Leena spoke softly. "It's obviously Monday, but what time?"

"A little after noon."

"Don't you think we should be heading to the precinct?"

"Considering Captain Sommers in on vacation and you are basically acting captain, I don't really think anyone is going to say anything."

"I guess you drive a good point. I'd still like to go in and check up on the place. I have this awful feeling that something happened over the weekend, Philip related," she looked around the dank basement.

"I agree, but first I vote we get you to feeling better. Give you an hour? That should be enough time to get dressed, eat and finish healing."

Hopping up the stairs, James gently pushed open the door. Hearing Matt, Samuel, and Raphael conversing, Leena threw on her clothes, using the pillar to help her stand. Feeling her strength come back, she grabbed the railing, making her way slowly up the staircase. Kicking open the door, she was greeted once again with the blinding light of the winter afternoon. Shielding her eyes, Leena slowly made her way to the group of guys sitting around the table. Chatter and the sound of glasses connecting with the table filled the room.

Sliding a warm flask of Dr. Plasma in Leena's direction, Raphael gave a smile, winking. Knowing it would be quick to give her strength, she chugged down her drink. She resembled someone who had run a marathon and needed to replenish with a fresh, cold glass of water. Filled with breakfast, they began to gather their belongings.

"Stop!" Raphael whispered; a harshness filled his word. His eyes searching the place.

"What now?" a collective sigh filled the bar.

"We're not alone," he spoke, lowering his voice, pushing the group to the counter.

"What the hell do you mean?" Leena pushed him away.

Before Raphael had a chance to speak, a large, husky man stepped from behind the stage curtains. The man, who allowed his stomach to protrude from under the bottom of his shirt, slowly made his way to center stage. Keeping an attentive eye on each of them, he gave an eerie smile. Standing their ground, Matt allowed his claws to extend, Leena's fangs grew, James slowly placed a hand on his gun and Samuel stood with confidence. Unwilling to attack before they received answers, they allowed the man to make his way to the edge of the stage.

"I wouldn't try anything stupid," the man spoke, his voice raspy.

"Oh?"

"I have strict orders to kill the werewolf," he pointed his gun at Matt.

"From?" Leena barked, she grew more and more pissed with each passing second.

"A friend," the plump man cocked the gun.

"There's no reason for you to do this!" James made a feeble attempt at reasoning with the man.

Focusing harder on the large man, Leena saw his eyes were glazed over, zombie like. Knowing this was connected with Philip, Leena's entire expression changed. Taking a slow step from the group, she kept a watchful eye on the stranger.

"Leena! Don't!" Samuel grabbed her arm.

Ripping her arm away from him, she took a few steps closer. Firing his gun in the air, he forced Leena to freeze. A few more warning shots were let loose, bullets punching holes in the ceiling. Raphael looked up; anger struck him as he saw multiple holes where his bedroom floor should be.

"Dammit!" Raphael whispered. "I just put that carpet in."

"Now's not the time for jokes," Samuel gave a sharp elbow to Raphael's side.

"If I don't kill the wolf, he'll kill me," the man spoke, almost trembling.

"He? He who?" Leena pressed on, carefully interrogating the man, being sure to not allow the group the knowledge that she already knew.

"It's of no matter to you, you bitch," the man spoke as if he didn't have control of his words.

Standing her ground, Leena was careful not to anger the man. Beads of sweat formed on the fat man's forehead, slowly running down his chubby face. The man shook with fear and determination, Leena, Matt, and Raphael could smell the odor that the rather sizeable man was producing. If they had to guess, he didn't shower for almost a week, he was rancid, and it was torture to their senses. How anyone could be around him was a mystery, hell they didn't even want to deal with him.

"The wolf must die, you must feel all the pain I have felt!" the man screamed, extending his arm further, steadying himself to kill Matt.

He was quick, Leena had no time to react, the man placed pressure on the trigger. James was quick to place himself between Matt and the bullet. Closing his eyes, James whispered into Matt's ear, letting him know how much he loved him. The room was filled with an unusual tense energy. With everyone looking to James, they witnessed something unexplainable. A ball of pale blue light erupted from James, near his core. The energy quickly expanding into a sphere, soon flew throughout the room. Throwing everyone in different directions, all but Matt and James were tossed against the walls, chairs, and tables.

The large man was tossed to the ceiling, colliding with beams above the stage. Leena, who was trapped under a broken table, found herself tossing pieces of metal and wood off her body. Samuel and Raphael poked their heads up from behind the bar, brushing pieces of broken glass off their shoulders, shaking dust from their hair. Leena looked around the bar, noticing Matt was on his knees, holding James in his lap. Slowly standing up, blood poured from all their wounds. Making her way to James, she saw his chest was slow to rise and just as slow to fall. Relieved that her friend was still alive, she looked to the stage.

"Where the fuck did he go?" she punched one of the few still intact pillars.

"Leena?" Raphael slowly walked to her, placing a gentle hand on her shoulder.

"Back off!" she tore away, glaring at him in a threatening way, indicating her willingness to fight whoever crosses her path.

"Look up, damn you!"

Spinning away from Raphael, Leena looked to where he had his hand extended. To her happiness, Leena saw the fat man had become entangled in the wires, a large electrical wire had wrapped around his neck. Slightly swinging back and forth, the unknown man was hanging lifeless, the wires and collision had killed the man, snapping his neck. The force of him connecting with the bars above caused numerous lacerations. Hitting one of the bars at great speed caused such damage that the man's head was ripped open, pieces of skull missing, leaving blood to cover the floor beneath him. Continuing to watch the man, Leena saw his jaw slowly fall open and something small fall out. Kneeling to see what it was, she saw with great disgust that the man had bit his tongue clean off. Knowing it was because of the impact, she smiled.

"Looks like even in death he won't be telling his tale," Raphael laughed.

"Knock it off!" Samuel barked, throwing a piece of rubble, striking Raphael hard in the head.

Quick to spin on his heels, he glared at Samuel, placing a hand to the back of his head. Seeing that Samuel drew blood, his eyes grew dark, fists began to clench. Fueled by anger, he lunged over a pile of broken tables, pinning Samuel to the ground.

"You think you're so goddamn tough, act all macho for Leena!"

"At least I can grab her attention! She doesn't look at me like I am a helpless puppy! All you Phoenix are the same!" Raphael drove a swift fist to the side of Samuels head; blood flew from his broken nose.

"What? You think because you have fucked her a few times that she will always come crawling back to you?" he shook the pain away as he drove a hard knee to Raphael's groin.

Ignoring the pain, Raphael was sure to keep Samuel in place. "Well look around, dick! She lives here now; you couldn't even attempt that in your wildest dreams!"

Samuel's anger began to grow, like an unattended forest fire. Grabbing Raphael's shoulders, he flipped him over, placing himself on top. Gaining the advantage, he threw punch after punch to each side of Raphael's face. With each hit, blood would spew from his nose, mouth and lacerations caused by the forceful punches. Seeing the weakness in Raphael's eyes, Samuel slowly stood up, Raphael's neck firmly grasped in his hand. Looking around the room, Samuel was hastily looking for anything he could use to harm Raphael further. Seeing the coat hooks on the wall, he walked over slowly, raised Raphael a few feet in the air and thrust him onto the splintered, wooden hooks.

With widened eyes, he looked at Samuel who in that moment had a frightening smile on his face. Feeling the hook graze his heart, Raphael let out a horrifyingly hair-raising scream, filled with pain. Water trickled from his eyes. How could he do this? Why? Raphael thought. Looking around the room, he saw Leena charge in their direction. Allowing himself enough energy to watch Leena throw Samuel across the bar, he smiled, the pain soon rendered him unconscious.

19

"I don't give a shit; you shouldn't have done that! What the hell was going through your mouse sized brain?" Raphael could hear Leena's voice fill the room.

"He was! I mean come on, really, that guy!"

"Samuel, what do you mean "that guy" are you really that jealous?"

"Jealous? No, I am not jealous of that guy!" Samuel's voice echoed.

Gaining strength to sit up, Raphael looked to the clock. With the day gone, he knew Leena didn't make it to work. Tilting his neck to the side, he felt the bones snap back into place. Letting out a small wince of pain, Leena was brought to a halt mid rant. Rushing to his side, she slowly pushed him back on the bar, lifting his shirt, checking his wounds. Being as careful as she could, she rolled him on his side, looking over the wounds inflicted from the hooks.

"You're not healing. Why?"

"I haven't fed. I think there may be a few splinters of wood left. I'm only glad that it can't kill me."

"You know, I have been a vampire for over one thousand years and a hybrid for just shy of a month. I will never understand how wood to the heart doesn't kill us," Leena laughed softly, running a damp rag over his wounds.

"Then what kills you? Just so I can remember for next time!" Samuel chimed in with anger and annoyance.

"Definitely not you, worthless weasel!" Raphael laughed, choking on blood.

"Enough!" She slapped Raphael across the head. "As for you, we die if decapitated and the head and body are buried in different, blessed cemeteries, weakened greatly if stabbed in the heart. There is probably a long list of different things that kill vampires, one of which is the sickness. Samuel you should know this, now get over here!" she demanded.

"What?" he hesitantly walked to Leena's side.

Approaching Leena, he was unaware of what happened as he was filled with great pain as she grabbed his hand, sliced it open with a shard of glass and placed it over Raphael's mouth. Unable to pull away, he scratched and punched Leena's hand, trying everything he could not to be dinner. Sinking his teeth into Samuel's hand, Raphael made sure to give an eerie smile while looking at him. Screeching in pain, Leena knew that Samuel had been through enough. Tossing him aside, she looked at the bloodied man on the table, witnessing a few of the wounds beginning to close.

"Sorry," she looked to Samuel.

"Bite me!" he gently rubbed the pain away.

"Looks like we have a long night ahead of us," she brushed dust from Raphael's face. "I've got a few splinters I need to remove, deep ones."

"What about me?" Samuel put his hand in the air, wound gaped open and blood still pouring like a small water fountain.

"You can leave."

"Like hell I will, I have no intention of leaving you with him!"

Ignoring the defeated man on the floor, she mumbled to herself. Clearly irritated, she had no problem grabbing a knife and cutting the splinters from Raphael's body. Not a single clean cut had taken place, and Leena didn't really care. With her focus being broken by the doors, she looked to see as James and Matt walked out of the darkness into the dim light of Eternal Night. Placing dinner on one of the few, still intact tables, they looked around the chaotic room.

"Look who's awake," James laughed.

"Where is Samuel?" Matt spoke, looking to Leena.

"I'm over here," a defeated voice came from behind the bar.

"The hell are you doing down there?" James laughed, spitting his soda across the room.

"Leena fed me to Raphael," still defeated, he ducked back behind the bar.

"Kinky," Matt joined James in his laughter.

With jerks for friends, Samuel raised his good hand and gave the group a stern middle finger. Laughing, both James and Matt ignored the group, ripped open the pizza boxes and gorged on delicious food from the Hometown Pizzeria. Grease poured from the corners of their mouths as they smacked their lips, unwilling to close their mouths while they ate. It was typical for a werewolf to eat voraciously after a shift as it takes a huge amount of energy. As for James, he just liked his food. Continuing to focus on tending the multiple wounds that were not yet healed, she was careful to not cause any further pain to Raphael.

Maybe I do have some feelings towards Raphael, but I find myself thinking of Samuel as well, as much as I hate to admit it. Leena thought to herself as she looked down at his slow healing body.

"What's on your mind, love?" Raphael smiled, pain still flowing through his body.

"Nothing really, other than the fact that you're a really lucky man."

"How so?"

"When Samuel is as pissed off like he was earlier, placing someone on wooden hooks isn't really his go to move."

"And what is?" Raphael inhaled deeply, grunting as his body ached.

"Ripping limbs off, ripping hearts out, basically he loses all control. If you didn't know what he was, you'd think he might be a Nightwalker," Leena explained, being careful to not alert Samuel, she failed.

"You're aware I can hear you, right?" Samuel poked his head up; anger and frustration filled his face. "Look man, if I wanted to kill you, believe me, you'd be dead!"

"Just hide back behind the bar and shut up!" Leena tossed a dirty rag at Samuel who quickly dodged and with another middle finger in the air, he disappeared.

"Not many of them running around anymore, are there?" Raphael slowly sat up. Growing tired of laying down, he knew that even in pain he needed to stretch.

"Nope, that's actually something none of us have been able to figure out," she pondered, looking out the window. "After the Anti Vampire Association was wiped out, they just vanished."

"I don't think that's something we will ever know," James chimed in, food particles flew from his mouth.

"Babe? James, close your mouth, you're not an animal!" Matt tossed a napkin at his face. "Who wiped out the AVA?"

"Vampires, other supernatural beings. In my opinion, I think they just began to fear for their lives and decided to disband," Leena spoke with confidence. "After the death of old man Shayla, as you know, James made a feeble attempt to hunt them down."

Finishing up their dinner, both James and Matt decided that it was time to head home. Opening the double doors, they saw a random box, no return address or anything. Calling to Leena, they placed it on a table. Worried, Raphael accompanied Leena to the box, hoping it wasn't another surprise.

"If this is a fucking head in a box, I'm going to be pissed!"

"I'm really happy I wasn't the only one who thought that," Raphael laughed.

The five of them stood around the box. Wonder filled the minds of James, Matt, and Samuel, as worry filled the thoughts of Leena and Raphael. Using a nail from the debris, Leena ran it across the top of the box. Slowly opening the package, they were all forced to take a step back as the rancid smell filled the room. Holding their breath, they braved the box once more. To both Leena and Samuel's dismay, they recognized what was in the box. The eyes, hands, a few innards, the fangs, and the nametag of the young vampire Justin Kelly, who worked at the Claresville Café.

"Dammit!" Samuel barked, slamming his fist on the table.

"That son of a bitch!" Leena's voice shook the room.

"Leena! Who is it? What is it?" both James and Matt spoke in unison, a pinch of sorrow filled their words, their hands still covering their nose and mouth.

"Justin Kelly, a young vampire from Claresville. He worked at the café. Seemed like such a good kid! Damn Philip, I hate him!" Leena barked, her voice shook not with sadness but with disgust and loathing.

Grabbing the box, Leena took the nametag and fangs which were tangled in innards and blood, placed them on the bar and made way to the kitchen. Igniting the large pizza oven, she looked down at the box, tears began to well in her eyes. With anger taking first place in her mind, she found herself allowing sadness to take a turn.

The hell is wrong with me? She thought, using her free hand to rub the tears from her eyes.

"Hey, you okay?" Samuel, Raphael, James, and Matt all spoke, checking up on their friend.

"Get the hell out! Get out now!" Leena stormed to the kitchen door, slamming it in their faces, shaking the frame.

Shocked at Leena's actions, the four guys sat at the bar, all grabbing drinks to numb the pain. With Leena in the kitchen, she once again set her focus on the box with the few remains of the departed, young vampire. Placing the box in the large stove, she watched as flames began to consume the outside, slowly peeling away at the layers of cardboard. The stove sizzled as blood trickled off of the wire rack and cleaned what was being scorched to the bottom. Watching what was left of the young vampire, Leena found herself falling to her knees, sorrow consumed her thoughts and tears streamed down her cheeks. Losing control, she placed her hands over her eyes, crying, trying to keep as quite as possible.

"Well, that stove should be fun to replace," Raphael spoke softly, being sure to alert everyone he was attempting to be funny.

"Probably going to shut down for a while. At least until you can get this place fixed up," Matt said tossing back a shot of vodka.

"Thankfully, I have insurance, not sure I have the money to replace all this."

The men continued their conversation as Leena kept to herself in the kitchen. Placing a chair under the handle, she hindered anyone from bothering her. Still sobbing, Leena looked for anything to wipe her eyes. As she found herself surrounded by paper towel, she came up empty handed. Using her sleeve to wipe away her sorrow, she grabbed a bottle of liquor from the counter, leaned against the cupboards and chugged. As a hybrid, her tolerance for alcohol was rather high. Knowing it would take a lot, she searched for more, she needed to numb the pain. Leena couldn't figure out why or how Philip had the ability to know her small connection to Justin Kelly.

How the hell did he know I had met this kid? Why did he target him? She thoughtfully whispered to herself. I swear I'm going to kill him.

Realizing in the time she had lost herself on the floor, she noticed that three empty bottles of rum were scattered around her. Looking to the clock, she noticed that it wasn't even close to midnight. As all the rum was gone, she stumbled across the kitchen, turned the knobs in the off position and leaned softly against the counter. Unable to shed anymore tears, she found herself gaining the courage to show herself to the guys. Scooting the chair from the door, she gently placed a foot at the base, lightly kicked it open and fell into disheveled room. Rushing to her side, James and Matt helped her to the bar, pulled up a chair, placed a glass of water within arm's reach and placed a cool rag to her forehead.

"So, an hour and a half in the kitchen. You reek of liquor and I have never seen your eyes this puffy. You fine to talk?" James pressed her for information.

"No!" she remained stern, keeping total anger at bay.

Recognizing her body language, James sat himself back at the bar, reached for another beer and leaned against Matt. With still watery eyes, she looked to the couple and smiled. Knowing that was something she would never have; her smile was quickly taken over by an exhausted expression. With the clock chiming, telling everyone it was ten-o-clock, they ignored the time and poured another round of drinks. Leaving Leena out of the round of shots, they chose to slide her a flask of Dr. Plasma, hoping it would boost her energy. If nothing more, they hoped it would allow her to feel better.

20

With the night passing by and early morning making its way through the windows, the bar was filled with bright, unforgiving light. The sky filled the windowsills with snow and blanketed the Earth overnight. Shielding their eyes from the harsh sun, the group filled the bar with moans and the occasional whine as their heads throbbed from the prior night's drunkenness. Leena, as she was cut off earlier than the rest, found herself feeling rather pleasant. Looking around at her friends, she quietly laughed to herself. Her laughter was brought to a halt as she was quick to notice the absence of Samuel. Allowing the group time to gather themselves, Leena quietly looked around the bar. Unable to find any signs of Samuel, she quietly opened the exit, allowing the room to flood with the chilled November wind. Tossing on her jacket, she stepped outside, looking for tracks that would lead to the missing man.

Spending sometime outside, she listened to the early morning sounds that accompanied the busy Coleman lifestyle. Cars honked on their way to work, people filled the sidewalk as they walked from small business to small business and the wind whistled through the naked, ice covered trees. With no luck of finding Samuel, she made her way back into the warmth of Eternal Night. Shaking the snow from her jacket, she tossed it on the table, slapped her hand on the table causing enough commotion to wake the dead.

"Wake up!"

"Leena, sweetie, why?" Raphael, James, and Matt all spoke in unison, various stages of exhaustion and hungover looks filled their faces.

"Samuel is gone! Did anyone see where he went?" her tone hurried; a hint of annoyance pressed through her words.

"Jesus! Relax, would you? He left crazy late last night," James stumbled to the coffee maker.

"To go where? Spill!"

"Home, damn! Said he wanted to get a jump on all this bullshit."

"And you believed him?" Leena searched for her phone. "He's a Phoenix with a fiery temper. He hates Philip almost as much as I, he felt for the kid who arrived here in a box when we met him in Claresville and in general, life seems to be smacking him in the face," she spoke as the search for her phone came to an end.

"So, what's your plan then?" Raphael slowly made way in her direction.

Ignoring her friends, she swiped vigorously across her phone screen. Pressing hard on Samuel's name, she placed the phone to her ear, listening to it ring. With no sign of Samuel picking up his phone, she impatiently waited for the voicemail notification.

"Samuel! Where the hell are you? I'm not an idiot, I know you didn't go home to get a good start on the day! Call me back as soon as you get this!" Leena barked her message into the phone.

"The three of you should go to the precinct and look for Samuel. I'll get this place cleaned up. It's still going to be a while before I can open up again," Raphael spoke softly, slightly upset about the previous events.

While James and Matt stepped to the side and called a taxi, Leena packed up a few of her scattered belongs. Throwing on her jacket, she grabbed the back of Raphael's head, pulled him close and planted a long passionate kiss to his lips. Finishing up the request of taxi service, James and Matt looked to Leena, confusion filled their faces. Ignoring her random act of passion, they stepped outside, leaving Leena to catch up.

"I know I shouldn't ask, but why?"

Inhaling deeply, she looked him in the eyes, placed a hand to his cheek and cracked a crooked smile. "Don't look too much into it. Okay?" she turned from him while simultaneously slapping the side of his head.

Smiling, Raphael made his way to the kitchen. Leaving the bar, she stepped into the cold winds that whipped its way between the buildings. Disregarding the gaze that came from her friends, she leaned against the tree, awaiting the arrival of the taxi. They knew it was going to be a cold day as the sun was unwilling to show itself.

"If you would kindly stop gawking at me, that would be much appreciated."

"Sorry," James and Matt laughed as they huddled close to keep warm.

"What's with taxis taking forever? Hasn't anyone ever heard of Uber?" Leena tried desperately to change the subject. "I can only assume they would work faster."

Spending a moment to continue her rant, she was soon cut off as the taxi made its way in their direction. Cramming into the car, James tapped the window, flashed his badge indicating to the driver of where they needed to be. Speeding away from Eternal Night, Leena subtly looked back to the bar, noticing that Raphael was standing in the window looking down to her. Embarrassment began to flood over Leena, forcing her to spin her head back to her friends. Don't think too much of it. Leena thought to herself. There is no way anyone can love you, there is no way you can love anyone.

With the King of Coleman miles away, Leena felt the ability to breathe easy once again. Occasionally checking her phone for any updates from Samuel, she would let out a casual sigh of despair as no information presented itself.

"Oh, little heads up, Matt and I are getting married on the 30th."

"That seems a little quick. Don't you think?" Leena spoke carefully, not wanting to upset one of her best friends.

"When you know, you know," Matt smiled, giving James a gentle kiss on the cheek. "Plus, the captain will be back from vacation that day, and she has apparently been excited for this moment."

"Well I sure hope this is all taken care of by then. I really don't feel like dealing with missing friends, a psychopathic killer and anything else that is going on."

The driver pulled up to the precinct, slapped a few buttons, unlocking the doors. Matt tossed some cash to the driver as they all fell out of the vehicle. Simultaneously letting out a large sigh, they made their way into the building. Their ears soon filled with officers talking, people in handcuffs screaming, chairs scratching the wooden floors and pens clicking as the occasional officer sat irritated taking notes over the phone.

An officer behind the counter recognized Leena and James, quickly gathered their mail and any other messages they may have missed in their absence. Thanking the newbie officer, Leena flipped through her mail, pressing the elevator button with her elbow. Waiting for the ride to their office, James and Matt spoke quietly about the upcoming wedding, as Leena was left to think about Raphael and their kiss. Interrupted by the ring of the elevator, they stepped into the metal box, Matt pressed the button and the doors slowly shut them in. "I wonder what Raphe is up to," Leena found herself once again thinking of the kiss.

21

At Eternal Night, Raphael found himself sweeping up bits of glass, screws, and splinters of wood. Tossing larger pieces into various garbage cans. Looking up to the stage, he saw the dangling corpse of the random attacker slowly swinging from side to side. Placing the broom against a pillar, he walked up to the stage, played with the wires for a bit and watched as the lifeless, tongueless man fell to the floor into the pool of his own blood. Kneeling down to grab the man by his shoulders in an attempt to drag him off the stage, Raphael heard the screeching of the doors.

"Sorry we're closed, I must've forgot to lock the door," he spoke quickly tossing a curtain over the body.

"Oh, my friend, there is no need to hide the body," a familiar voice pierced his ears.

"Sorry?" Raphael spoke, spinning quickly on his heels. Making eye contact with Samuel, who wasn't alone. "Where the hell have you been? And who the hell are you?"

"Apologies, it has been a while since we have seen each other. Hasn't it?"

"No!" Raphael's voice was suddenly filled with terror and dread.

"That's the face I have grown to love."

"Philip, what the hell are you doing here?"

"I'm taking what I want. I told my dear sister that I want to be king, and I want her to spill all the truth she has been hiding from everyone!"

"Fuck you! Get out of my bar!" Raphael barked, his fangs grew, and eyes darkened.

He readied himself for battle, looking between Samuel and Philip. If I have to kill Samuel, this will kill Leena! Raphael thought, his mind burned at the possible realization. Keeping an eye on them, he took a few slow steps to the front of the stage. A broken board was close to his foot, with a quick glance he kicked the board at Philip, screws out. Dodging the board, he snapped his fingers, sending Samuel into a violent rage. Jumping over debris, he lunged in Raphael's direction, anger filling his mind. Noticing the zombie like expression on his face, Raphael stepped aside just in time to miss the knife hidden in Samuel's hand. Hastily picking up a plank, he brought the board up, connecting hard with Samuel's jaw. Samuel was left hanging half off the stage, lights out at last, or so Raphael thought. Grabbing Raphael by the throat, Samuel slowly lifted him in the air, leaving his feet to search for the safety of the floor. Choking, he grabbed Samuel's hand, placed a foot on his abdomen, twisted his wrist and pressed off, freeing himself from Samuel's deadly grasp. Landing in the pile of nails and splinters, Raphael looked up to meet the eerie, yellow-orange eyes and unearthly gaze of Philip. Attempting to escape, he leaned back, piercing his hands with the loose screws and shards of wood. Brushing the dust off his clothing, Samuel rushed in Raphael's direction, ready for another devastating attack.

"Enough!" Philip again snapped his fingers, forcing Samuel to an immediate stop. "That is all."

"What are you waiting for?"

"My old friend, I'm not waiting for anything. I have everything right where I want it!" Philip spoke, raising a hand in the air. With a quick gesture he brought a hard hand down, slapping Raphael across the face, blood spewed from his mouth.

"You're just as pathetic as ever! If Leena were to find out that I have known you long before this, she would kill us both. So, just get it over with!"

"No, no, no! I have told my sister that I want to be king, she knows the truth she must reveal. I have sworn eternal hatred towards her. Blackmail is my specialty, and I will make her life a living hell!" Philip spoke, kneeling to meet Raphael. "I'm going to have a lot of fun. This city and all the poor souls in it will be mine! I think I will start with this worthless bar."

"I'll be damned if I let you take the bar, my home!" Raphael barked, his wounds causing him to howl in pain.

Using his less bloodied up hand, he tossed dust and splinters in Philip's face. Falling on his back, he found Raphael pounced on top of him. Attempting to snap, Philip was soon filled with pain as Raphael shoved a large piece of wood into his hands, pinning him to the floor.

"Let's see you call your attack dog now!"

No actions, no words left Philip's body, when soon Raphael was thrown across the room. Pulling the wood from Philip's hands, Samuel stood inhaling and exhaling deeply. Standing their ground, Philip and Samuel lowered their bodies, preparing to charge. Within a split second the three men all charged; Samuel fell to the floor as if sliding into home base. Tripping Raphael, who was now midair, soon found himself locked in Philip's arm. Spinning him around, he brought him above his head and with a swift motion, he slammed Raphael into the floor, headfirst. The room was filled with the cracking of bones and splat of blood as Raphael's head quickly split open upon contact. Seemingly lifeless on the floor, both Philip and Samuel stood victorious.

"Tie him up, douse the ropes in a hawthorn and water solution!" Philip spoke, tossing the ropes in Samuel's face.

As Raphael was being taken care of, Philip struck a match, tossing it on the body of the man on the stage. Leaving Samuel to take care of the flames and remains of the large man, Philip searched for his phone. Calling his team of compelled pets, Philip ordered for his belongings to be brought to Eternal Night. Samuel, who had finally finished taking care of the burning body, eyed Philip.

"What?" he looked to the Phoenix. "Got something to say?"

Samuel remained silent, gazing at Philip. Still hanging on to what he could of his humanity, he tore his gaze away from Philip, continuing to tend to Raphael's unconscious body. Having no choice in his actions, Samuel was forced to not only watch Raphael, but also tidy up the bar. Occasionally glaring at Philip, he noticed some time had passed by. With the large clock chiming twelve times, they were alerted that noon had finally approached. Fixing Raphael's ropes, Samuel's attention was brought to the bar doors as the hinges screamed and the outside light caused the small group of people entering to look like dark silhouettes.

"Austin, Megan, welcome to our new home!" Philip laughed hauntingly.

The two stepped into the light, just as Raphael was beginning to recover consciousness. Seeing the blurred outlines, Raphael did everything he could to shake away the awful feeling he had in the pit of his stomach. Witnessing a zombie like expression on their faces, he knew something was wrong, he didn't care for the feeling that came next. Son of a bitch! Raphael thought to himself. Philip has complete control of them.

Looking around the bar, Raphael was grasped firmly by the neck, Philip placing him face to face. Gazing deep into his eyes, Philip focused on Raphael, bringing him to the same zombie like trance that Austin, Megan, and Samuel were prisoners of. Trying to mentally fight off Philip's compulsion, Raphael closed his eyes tight. Growing angered, Philip thrust a fist into Raphael's chest, causing him to wrench his body in pain, widening his eyes, allowing Philip access into his mind.

"Forget your friends, forget Leena, you belong to me now! You will bow to me, work for me, kill for me!" Philip spoke calmly, but assertively.

His eye glossed over, his breath steadied, and body relaxed. Raphael was no longer tense, no longer afraid. Feeling at ease, Philip ordered for the restraints to be taken away, allowing Raphael some freedom. Lining up his minions, his attention was brought to Raphael's blaring phone. Ripping the device from his pocket, he looked at the number, laughed, sat on his throne, brought the phone to his ear, and spoke.

"Morning, Leena," Philip filled her ears with an unearthly tone.

"What the hell did you do to Raphael?"

"My new pet? He is quite a wonderful addition to my collection," he laughed. "Everyone, please say hello to my sister, Leena?"

"Hello!" various, yet quite recognizable voices filled Leena's head.

Her eyes widened as she could make out not only Megan's voice, but Samuel and Raphael's voice as well. The fourth was a bit foggy for her. Placing the phone on speaker, she granted James and Matt the ability to hear the call as well.

"That's Austin, Mark's cousin!" James whispered, being careful to not alert Philip of their presents.

Leena's brow slowly began to rise, her jaw dropped. The news shot through her head like a BB in a bucket. Wishing that Mark was with them, Leena kept the phone on speaker.

"Leena, by now I am sure that you have discovered the hidden message in the blackmail letter. I've already begun to claim Coleman for my own. I'll never stop hating you, even when I have it all, I'll still swear eternal torture on you! Have you decided to speak the truth?"

"Enough!" Leena barked. "Shut up!"

More laughter flew through the speakers, an evil cackle. Clicking the end button, Philip tossed the phone on the table, looked at Raphael and smiled, eerily. Leaving Leena on the other end feeling lost. Placing himself just a few inches away from Raphael's face, he muttered a few words that seemed to activate him, placing himself in a robotic state. With the group of various supernatural beings all standing at attention, Philip began to pace back and forth.

22

Standing in the middle of the office, Leena was overtaken by the sounds of the precinct. Officers yelling, James and Matt talking about Philip and Mark, drunken idiots handcuffed to benches trying to get loose. The smell of coffee, instant heat burritos, doughnuts and even the stench of musky cologne attacked Leena's sinuses. All of her senses were being attacked and it just began to overload her. Pushing bluecoats and even senior officers out of her way, she charged towards the captain's office. Slamming the door behind her, she locked the handle, grabbed a chair, and placed herself in front of the window.

What the hell am I going to do? She thought, looking out the window, watching the snow fall.

Looking to her phone, she found herself swiping through pictures of her, Raphael and even Samuel. Taking in the silence, she stood from the chair, pacing around the office. Doing what she could to stay calm, she found that each deep breath was forcing her to grow more and more angry. Throwing her fist into the wall near the entrance, she threw open the door, bellowing for James and Matt. Running to the office, they plowed through the door with worry in their eyes.

"What? What's wrong?" they spoke quickly.

"We need to take out Philip, soon!" she rushed around the office, gathering her jacket, leaving the keys to the car. Figuring that a quiet approach to Eternal Night would be the best.

"Leena! Dude you are freaking out!" James grabbed her shoulders, looking her in the eyes. "You can't go in halfcocked; he will obliterate you; he'll obliterate us!" he added.

"I for one choose life, thank you!" Matt threw in his opinion.

Taking time to wind down, they all sat around the desk, head in hands contemplating their next plan of action. The sound of heavy snow hitting the window blocked out the sounds of the various officers outside of the door. Dark clouds filled the sky forcing them to flip on the office lights and even the desk lamp.

"I wonder if we should get ahold of Mark?" James questioned quietly.

"Do you really think that is a good idea?" Matt placed a hand on his shoulder. "I know I haven't known him long, but he seems like the kind of guy that may do something rash."

Head on the desk, Leena raised her hand in the air, pointing at Matt. "Yup, you're right. I've known him for a long time, obviously, he would charge in there without a plan."

"I still think that we should at least call him here to the precinct."

Nodding her head to James, she grabbed her phone, slide her finger across Mark's name and placed the phone to her ear. Waiting impatiently for Mark to answer, she bopped up and down in her chair. Hearing the click of his phone, she perked up in the seat, preparing herself for the explosion.

"Hey! There's my best friend. How you been?" Mark's voice was filled with happiness.

"Um, I've been okay. Can't complain. Look, is there any way you could come on down to the precinct?" Leena was careful with her words.

"Yeah, I can be there in about thirty minutes. See you soon."

Ending the call, Leena let out a deep sigh, filled with stress. The three of them looked at each other, concern for Mark took over their expressions. With the snow growing heavier, they knew it was going to take him a while to arrive. Mark had always been a cautious driver, so much that he made it a point never go over the speed limit—ever. It was one of the few things that drove Leena nuts. Knowing the weather was going to force Mark to show up late, Leena, James and Matt decided to take a quick coffee break.

"Detective Rose! A moment, please?" an officer called to her from across the way.

Giving James a sigh of annoyance, she stepped aside, watching her friends head off to the breakroom. Leena hated when newbies would pull her to the side, it was always something that they could easily figure out. Watching the newbie skip towards her, she quickly shot a glance at him, forcing him to freeze mid stride.

"What is it, Officer Gnaw?" Leena spoke, glancing at the man's name clip, tilting her head in confusion at the name.

"You forgot a piece of mail. Pretty fancy if someone is using a black envelope. Don't you think?" he smiled, handing her the letter.

Leena's expression went from annoyance, to confusion, to anger within the blink of an eye. She knew what this was, but it felt heavier than the other envelope. Ignoring the officer in front of her, Leena pushed him to the side, crashed into the chair at her desk and searched for the letter opener in her mess of a drawer. Giving up, she swiftly ripped off the top off the letter. Looking into yet another blackmail letter from her brother, she tipped it over and watched as black rose petals fell from the envelope, falling on and over her desk.

"Leena, I have already won! I have Raphael, Samuel, Megan, and Austin! They are my pets, I have taken control of Eternal Night, you have no home! I'm growing impatient, Leena, speak the truth to your friends. NOW! There is no captain to help you. You feel like she thought about going on vacation alone? I planted that seed; she is gone because I made it so! You have no help, I am now the King of Coleman, and I always will be. You have until the wedding of Matt and James to give them who you truly are! Captain Sommers returns the 30th from her little trip. If you haven't given up who you are, I will kill her! Have a wonderful rest of your week, Leena. With great hatred, The Darkest Rose."

Leena mouthed the letter to herself, looking around the room, eyeing James in the breakroom who was pouring a newly brewed cup of coffee. Slamming her fists on the desk, rose petals scattered as the wind from the impact blew them in various directions. Hoping no one saw her, she gathered the petals as quick she could, tossed them in the trash and forced her expression to change from lost and angered to calm and collected. Praying that there was at least one Dr. Plasma in the breakroom, she stumbled to her friends in a way that would resemble someone who just broke their back moving sixty-four, fifty-pound bags of road patch. Leaning against the doorway, she eyed James, who in return looked her up and down. Knowing she was off, he rushed to her, held her up, signaled for Matt to bring a chair and placed her gently in the seat.

"You're terrible at hiding facial expressions," James looked into her tired eyes. "What happened?" James added as Matt ripped the top off of the flask of Dr. Plasma.

"Another goddamned letter!" she barked, tossing back the whole flask of Dr. Plasma. "That fucker sent me another blackmail letter!"

Taking the letter from her hand, both James and Matt moved their eyes over the words, silently reading the threatening note. Looking to each other, they held hands, eyes welled with tears. Shaking the sadness away, James held tight to Matt's hand, looked him in the eyes, kissed him sensually and glared to Leena.

"I get that he is your brother, but I've had it! We are going after him, Now!" James' voiced filled the room, seeming to shake the walls.

"I agree, love. Leena, what is he forcing you to say? Why is he giving you until our wedding? What did Sommers do?" Matt's voice trembled; his rugged manliness was beginning to slip away as tears fell down his cheeks.

A werewolf and a hard ass, at times. How could these emotions fuck with him so terribly? Although before anyone's wedding if they received a letter or even information such as this, it could screw with them. Hesitant to speak, Leena stood from the chair, embracing her friends. Gripping them tightly, she shook as she hugged them, unwilling for her friends to endure the pain that she has to deal with. How was she going to keep them safe without spilling the secret that Philip is demanding? If he knows, why isn't he doing anything about it?

"Matt, I don't know why I am being timed. I sure as hell will do my best not to lose another captain! Just, I need the two of you to understand that I can't say what he is demanding. Please?" Leena spoke softly. "We will take care of this all before she gets back," she added, though her thoughts were far different.

Taking some time to unwind in the breakroom, they looked to the clock. With Mark arriving any minute, they knew they needed to look as if they didn't spend the last half hour in distress. Tidying up the breakroom and office, they heard the elevator ding. Knowing it had to be Mark, they all quickly sat, perked up in the chairs, looking to the hallway. Strolling happily down the hallway, the only thought that crossed their minds as they watch him bob up and down was how someone in times like this can be so happy.

"Hey fellas, what's up?" Mark smiled, embracing the group.

Pulling away, Leena looked to Mark, her head filling with sorrow as she knew what needed to come next. Signaling for him to sit, they all pulled up their chairs, looking to one another. James and Matt couldn't hold in the emotions. Losing control, they lost their shit as tears once again streamed down their faces. Confused, Mark placed a gentle hand on both men, looked them in the eyes and raised a brow.

"Just tell me. What happened?" Mark gripped their hands tighter.

"No! I mean, I'll tell him. It should come from me."

Nodding in approval, they pulled their hands from Mark's grasp, walking away from the table, through the door to another room. Eyeing his best friend, Mark began to open his mouth, placing her hand in the air, he stopped, prohibiting any words to fall from his lips. Growing worried, he looked to Leena with a furrowed brow. Encouraging him to sit closer, she gave him a hard, long look, deep into his eyes.

"Scaring me," he spoke, drawing out the word scaring, trying to ease the tension.

"Look, Mark, I have something I need to say, but they have to stay between us for a while. Okay?" she spoke softly. "By no means can James or Matt know what I am going to tell you," she added, hoping for a positive reaction.

"Yeah, sure, whatever."

Filling her words with lies, she gave Mark the information she felt would best steer him away from Philip and finding out that Austin was still alive. She sure has hell wasn't going to spill her secret to anyone. Leena just needed to do her best in buying time, with high hopes that she could take out her brother on her own. Inhaling deeply, she smiled to Mark, which in turn as it always has done, forced him to smile right back.

"I received another blackmail letter from Philip. This time it didn't have anything to do with "speaking the truth". He decided that he was going to threaten Captain Sommers," she spoke, her words filled with lies which hurt her to do to Mark. Knowing the only truth was the threat to Sommers, she felt by the time this was all over, she was going to be one hell of a liar. If lying paid, she would be rich.

Mark was filled with a blank expression. It looked to Leena that he was attempting to figure out if she was lying. Silence filled the room; Leena couldn't even hear the heartbeat of any officers. Hoping for the best, she kept a strong gaze on Mark. Tearing away from Leena, she jumped in her seat, shocked at his actions. Flicking his hand in the air, a chair hovered away from the floor and with another flick, Leena saw the chair soar through the office, striking the far wall.

"Fuck him! We won't lose another captain!" Mark clenched his fists; smoke filled the space between his fingers as flames grew in the palms of his hands.

"Mark! Please?" she urged him to relax before any damage was done. "Sit down."

"No! I've had it! Luna, Bella, Austin, and threats, it's all too much! We're going to do something about this son of a bitch!" the smoke in his hands began to thicken.

"Calm down, now! No one is going to do anything about Philip. If we ignore him, he will fizzle out, grow bored and leave," more lies leapt from her lips.

"You said it yourself, that would never happen, Leena!"

"I was wrong, I just want you, James and Matt to ignore the thought of him, for me."

"What? So, you can have your lovers help you instead of your partner and best friend!" his temper began to flare.

"No, I am taking care of this by myself. Everything will be fine. You focus on Bella and our friends," more lies flew out, Leena didn't care, she was hoping to protect the ones she cared about.

Making the attempt to calm himself, Mark inhaled deeply, heavily forcing the air from his body after each inhale, causing a rather annoying, yet boisterous exhale. Pacing around the desk, he would occasionally eye Leena, the clock and even look for the rest of the gang. Stopping for a phone call, Leena took the opportunity to shoot a quick message to James and Matt, allowing them the knowledge that she informed Mark of everything. In the dark about Leena's lies, they made their way to her.

"James, Matt and Mark, I need you to follow a lead on a case. Just received an e-mail, I feel it will need all the expertise you three have."

"What about you?" they spoke in unison; Leena almost caught a hint of curiosity and disbelief of her words.

"I've got a shit ton of paperwork I need to do," Leena just spewed out lie after lie. It was almost a new talent she was developing. "I'll sit here and accomplish that; I feel you can handle a case without me. Can't you?"

"Of course," smiled Matt. Excitement filled his eyes as he very seldom got to go on a case without Leena.

James looked to her; total confusion struck him. "Leena, you never miss out on a case. Why is this different?"

"I just think it's time for me to get a few things done. I am always babysitting you guys. What is so wrong with me getting some work done?"

"Nothing, just new for you is all!" Mark laughed, tapping James on the shoulder, tilting his head, gesturing for them to follow. Watching out the window, Leena waited patiently for them to leave. Gathering what she needed, she peeked through the door, making sure that other officers weren't aware of her. Sneaking to the elevator, she placed a finger on the button, hesitant to make any noise, she chose the stairs to be a better fit.

I hate lying to them, but I need to protect everyone! She thought as she descended the stairs. Opening the double doors, she yet again made sure the coast was clear before rushing through.

23

Sneaking around Leena, they tucked behind the bushes, snow filled their hair as they watched her feebly attempt to sneak by them. Walking down the street, Mark, James, and Matt were careful to avoid being seen by Leena. Ducking in and behind snowbanks, they found following her to be harder than they thought. Watching as Leena would occasionally pull out her phone, they depended on Matt to use his superhuman hearing to eavesdrop on her multitude of conversations. Unable to figure out who she was talking to, they continued to follow, knowing all too well that they definitely looked like stalkers to any bystander.

"Look, I am on the way. I am alone," Matt relayed the information he was able to make out with his superhuman hearing.

"Who the hell do you think she is talking to?" Mark spoke, more curiosity filled than he was before leaving the precinct.

"Who do you think? Probably Raphael or Samuel. You know she has been choosing to see them more than she has chosen to be at work, or even help us?" James spoke, flailing his arms causing him to slip on some hidden ice.

Landing hard on the sidewalk, Mark and Matt quickly pulled him out of sight. Spinning quickly on her heels, Leena looked for the cause of commotion. With no time to spare, she looked back, gave up on whatever was making noise and began her journey once again. Quietly laughing, Matt was sure to ask if James was okay, knowing they needed to focus, they brushed him off, quickly following Leena. Being sure not to lose her, they did their best to dodge her view, dodge hidden ice and keep warm, which was easy for the werewolf, not so much for the others. Keeping close to Matt, James snuggled up for warmth. Mark snapped a finger, causing a small flame to ignite in his hands, keeping it hidden from the general public. The last thing that they needed was some dumbass calling them out.

Miles upon miles had passed when the three of them recognized the building that they were all approaching. As Eternal Night began to grow on the horizon, the three men all looked at each other. Brows raised; they knew that their suspicions were correct.

"I knew it!" Mark whispered harshly. "I knew she was going after Philip."

"What makes you say that?" James spoke, his words filled with anger.

"I know when my best friend is acting shifty! Leena was nowhere near her usual self."

"Or, and here is a crazy thought, maybe she is having a midday hookup with Raphael! Did you ever think of that?" James' eyes rolled; his lips pursed in annoyance.

"It has to be Philip! I am getting this horrible feeling. You know the one you get before disaster strikes? I'm telling you Leena has been hiding something. Trust me, it's a gift!"

"Okay! Fine! Say it is Philip, what then? Even more so, how did he get into Eternal Night? What would he need with a bar?"

Ignoring his fiancé and friend, Matt pointed an ear in Leena's direction, hoping to catch more evidence. Watching from the corner, they eyed Leena as she entered the building, leaving them in the dead silence of winter. "I hate to say this, I really do, but Mark was right. I was able to make out just one word from Leena before she entered, it was brother," Matt spoke softly, feeling let down. Eyes wide, they lost track of their thoughts, unable to move they stood in place as snow packed itself on their shoulders.

Brushing as much snow as they could from their jackets, they puffed out their chests, decided to go around back, to surprise Leena, and if Philip were present, attack. What could go wrong? A witch, werewolf and powerful fey, they had the upper hand, right? Using magic to silently pick the back lock, Mark waved his hand over the doorknob in various ways until a small click filled the silence. Preparing for the worst, they readied themselves for a fight, but nothing came.

"Way to be silent!" James lightly slapped the back of Mark's head.

"Hey! At least I could get us in."

Carefully pushing the door open, they listened for any signs of a struggle. The hinges began to scream, forcing them to stop before being noticed. Forcing his friends to take a step back, he placed his hands together in a prayer like fashion. Pulling his hands apart, the hinges slowly and quietly deconstructed themselves, pieces of metal hovered in the air. After releasing the door, it pulled away from the wall, lifting higher to avoid colliding with anything in the way. Breathing heavy, Mark did everything he could to keep not only himself quiet, but his spell as silent as possible. Quietly exhaling, he slowly pressed his hands together, which in turn allowed the door to pull itself back together and gently fall to the ground.

Looking at Mark, James and Matt eyed each other, eyes wide open, jaws falling to the ground. Forgetting how powerful Mark actually was, they shook off the amazement, gathered their thoughts and slowly entered Eternal Night. If anyone could help Leena, it would be her group of best friends and co-workers.

"So, we meet at last!" an eerie voice filled their ears.

Ducking under ropes and pipes, they ignored the voice, making their way to the stage. Hiding behind curtains, James, Mark, and Matt all carefully peeked around them, hoping they would stay unnoticed. Eyeing his cousin, Mark noticed Austin, his eyes grew warm, tears of hate and anger filled his head.

"No!" Mark did the best he could to keep quiet.

Using his werewolf strength, Matt placed a hand on Mark, holding him in place. Having no plan of attack, they knew it wasn't the right time to jump out of hiding. Water began to stream its way down Mark's face, his body trembled with sadness. The three of them felt lied to, their trust in Leena was gone. Betrayal filled their thoughts as silent emotions began to run wild. Hatred soon took over, forcing them to expose themselves. Running from the back of the stage, they in unison leapt towards Philip. Catching them off guard, Philip flicked a hand in the air, sending a wave of energy in their direction. Throwing them across the room in various ways, they all met the floor with a thunderous crash. The sounds of air being forced from their bodies filled Eternal Night.

"Well now!" Philip barked, looking to the three incapacitated men. "I feel like I am growing more and more pissed off with each passing second!" he added, his voice calmer than it should be. Readying himself for another attack, he chose to cross his arms, walk to the bar, and lean against the cold metal, which covered the edges of the wood. Wondering why he didn't attack, they did their best to stand, weak from the blast of energy, their knees shook as they steadied themselves.

"Come on, coward!" Mark bellowed, throwing his hand up, sending what looked like a wall of fire towards Philip. Charging to him, the wall struck the bar, no Philip in sight. Looking around, Mark soon felt a cold arm wrap around his neck.

"All these years and you don't think I would know each and every move you have?" Philip grasped tighter.

Close to snapping his neck, he was brought back to reality by the shrieking of his sister.

"Philip, no!" Leena screamed, her hand in the air practically begging for Mark's safety. "Let him go! This has nothing to do with them! Don't act like a child!"

"I am not a child! Nobody tells the King of Coleman what to do!" his voice deep with rage, a low throated growl escaped his lips.

Swiftly moving his arm, the room was filled with the sound of Mark's neck snapping. Releasing his body, they watched in horror as their friend's body fell lifeless to the floor. Looking to Philip, Leena clenched a fist. Consumed in anger, she charged her brother, leapt over his body, grabbed his head while simultaneously spinning, throwing him across the room. A quick snap of the fingers forced Samuel, Raphael, Austin, and Megan all from their zombie like state. Leaving Matt and James to focus on the others, Philip took Leena for himself. Pinning her against the wall, he leaned close to Leena, eyes fixed and determined.

"Tell them, bitch! Tell them what you have been hiding or I swear I will fucking kill them!" Philip pressed hard against her throat.

"I don't know what difference it will make! You're acting like a child. I did what I had to do! Why have you held this grudge for so long?" Leena's words were occasionally interrupted by a gasp for air. "My friends knowing the real me won't save you from being a whiny little asshole!"

"No, but it will leave you alone, friendless! Which is what I promised, to make you feel how I felt all those years! I promised I would make your life a living hell! I've spent years watching, making an army, and you will never rest. You will never catch me! I'm damn good at what I do, Leena!"

"Fuck you!" she spit in his face, forcing him to release her. "I will catch you and when I do, it will be the best day of my life, watching you suffer!"

Shaking his head, Leena knew that her words meant nothing. How could anyone take down a maniac such as Philip? Stumbling a few feet back, Leena looked to Matt and James who were doing whatever they could to hold the four attackers at bay. Matt, who clearly had enough of this, channeled his inner self, allowing the wolf within to emerge. Shifting from man to wolf, a howl filled Eternal Night. Placing himself between their attackers, he kept distance between James and danger. Fear filled the eyes of Samuel, Raphael, Megan, and Austin as even in the tranced state of mind, they knew better than to go against Matt. With a menacing snarl, he would force them to jump as a deep bark left his muzzle. Driving them into the kitchen, he allowed James to lock the door, leaving Philip without backup. Leaning against Matt, James knew that it would take a great deal of work for Matt to return to his old self. Making their way to Mark's side, they placed his head in James' lap, brushing dirt from his face.

Reaching to the floor, Leena quickly picked up a plank of wood from the pre destroyed bar. Charging at Philip, he was quick to dodge, rip the wood from her hands and spin, returning to Leena what would have been a devastating blow. The board connected hard with Leena's skull, pieces of wood scattered, forcing Matt and James to shield their eyes. Tearing her head open, blood poured from Leena's wound. Blinking rapidly, she tried her damnedest to regain focus, but it was too late. Philip was at this point a great deal faster and stronger than his sister. Grabbing her by the hair, Philip ripped her head back, removed a splinter of wood from the floor and plunged it deep into her neck. Knowing it wouldn't kill her, he laughed as he gained the upper hand. Choking on blood, Matt looked to the pain riddled Leena, bashed a paw to the floor, ready to attack.

Unwilling to lose him, Leena glared deep into Matt's eyes, forcing him to back down.

She gathered what energy she could, forcing herself to stand. Pulling the large splinter from her throat, she stumbled for a moment, looked to James and Matt, then back to Philip. His unearthly laughter filling the air.

"You want me to talk? Fine!" she stood on shaking legs, her strength nowhere to be found.

Before Leena had a chance to spill her secret, Philip was soon brought to his knees, wrapped in wires that hung from the ceiling and debris. Looking around, Leena saw Matt slowly shift back, James' eyes went wide as Mark was slowly sitting up, hand in the air. Their expression filled with shock.

"Please tell me you useless, sorry excuse for a hybrid, that you didn't think you could take me down by simply breaking my neck?" Mark laughed, brushing dust from his jacket. "Do you really think that I would enter any building without a resurrection spell placed on me? Really?"

Philip had no words, trapped in a web of wires, he continued to smile, eerily. Slowly walking up to the maniac, Mark placed his hands on Philip's temples, pressed hard and made a connection, hoping to reach the place in his mind where he kept control of Austin. A jolt of energy flew from Mark's fingertips to Philip's head as he found the connection. Releasing Austin and the others from compulsion, the room was filled with the pained scream of Philip as his control of them was burned away. Listening to the four bodies in the kitchen hit the floor, Leena knelt in front of Philip, a smile of victory stretched across her face.

"I told you, you fucker, that I would win!" Leena brought her fist in the air, cocked back, and connected hard with Philip's jaw.

The sound of cracking bones filled the bar, blood poured from the corner of his mouth. Falling to his side, a pool of his own blood began to form under him. Eyeing Leena, he continued to smile, unwilling to show pain. Letting out a ghostly laugh, Philip used the strength he could, brought himself to his knees, bowed his head and kept silent. Finding a spare set of cuffs, James rushed to Philip, hastily restricting Philip from doing any further damage once released from Mark's spell. Bringing him to his feet, the silence was broken as the door to the kitchen flew open. Raphael, Samuel, Megan, and Austin poured from the room, falling onto the floor of Eternal Night.

Calling a team to pick him up and escort him to the Coleman Police Department, Leena, James, and Matt gathered the rest of the group around a table. Looking around the group, she felt that Philip had no way to intervene, but felt hesitant on speaking a word. With late afternoon creeping in on them, Leena knew in her mind that she had no choice.

"Leena?" Mark spoke, arm wrapped around Austin as a smile and tears of happiness rolled down his cheek.

"I'm okay."

"No, you're not. You lied! About what? Who the hell knows? We are here to tell you that we are tired, tired of the lies, tired of you not being who you truly are!" Mark's voice shook, not with sorrow, but with anger.

"There are many reasons why I can't, and many reasons why I should. I'm sorry, I just can't say anything to anyone right now, not yet," she spoke, spinning away from the group as she heard the other officers' vehicles pulled up to the bar.

Leaving her group of friends, she pushed open the doors, filling the room with light and the cold breeze of November. The group was left looking to one another, confused and exhausted, some couldn't even remember the last few weeks. As Leena disappeared into the light of day, her place was soon taken by determined officers, showing off and hoping they would be recognized for bringing in Coleman's wandering killer.

24

Evening consumed the day, Matt, James, and Samuel met at the precinct, Austin, Megan, and Mark went home, Raphael vanished, and Leena locked herself in Captain Sommers office. With Philip locked up, Leena felt that she could breathe again. I have no idea how safe we are, no way of knowing if we can keep him trapped! Leena thought as she searched through her e-mails. With just a few days before the return of Captain Sommers, Leena tidied up the office, hoping that its cleanliness would hide the holes and tears in the walls. Approaching her desk, she saw Samuel sitting in her chair, a smile stretched across his face and a sparkle in his eyes.

"What do you want?" Leena made a feeble attempt to hide her happiness in Samuel being okay.

"Honestly? The truth. All your crazy brother kept talking about was the excitement about being King of Coleman and something about not being able to wait until that bitch is alone, when she speaks the truth. I would really love to know what that means?" he questioned, his posture poised, and eyes filled with determination as he watched her happiness for his safety fade away.

Thinking of ways to avoid his question, Leena looked around the office, for anything that needed her attention. Of course, nothing was wrong, the one time she needed something to happen, it didn't. Pushing Samuel from her chair, she quickly took his place, eyeing him up and down, stalling. Drawing random lines on a pad of paper, Leena played with a pen, every so often pressing the button, filling the silent room with annoying clicking sounds. Lightly tapping her fist on the table, Samuel was startled at the random act.

"I'm sick and tired of everyone thinking that I have something to hide!" her voice carried through the office, alarming innocent people.

"Really?" Samuel spoke, rage filling his spirit. "For someone who has nothing to hide, you get pissed off quite easily!" his anger was beginning to grow uncontrollable.

"Stand down! I don't want to hurt you!" Leena stood, ready to defend herself if necessary.

"Of all the people you can trust, it should be me. I know I have made mistakes in the past, but I have been the truest friend you have ever had!"

"Wrong!" Leena cut him off, her fists clenched. Unwilling to deal with Samuel's uncontrollable anger. "Mark has been my closest friend, he never abandoned me, never left without saying goodbye!" she added, her eyes welled as feelings for Samuel grew uncontrollable.

Leaving Samuel speechless, she tore herself from his presence, heading to her brothers' cell. Standing alone at Leena's desk, he looked around the precinct as officers looked at him with shocked expressions. Heading to the breakroom, Samuel ignored the whispers of others. Approaching the cells, Leena swiped her badge through the control unit, pressed a few buttons and walked in, slowly. Checking each cell, she looked hastily for Philip. Hearing his unearthly laugh, she rushed to the back of the room, looking through the last set of bars. Philip, who was sitting at the edge of the bed, hands cuffed together was laughing, louder and louder. Punching his cell door, Leena brought Philip to an abrupt halt in laughter.

"Good evening, Leena. How are you feeling?"

"Happy, that you're behind bars."

"No worry at all? It doesn't cross your mind that I may not be here for long?" Philip spoke with ease.

"I've got guards watching this place twenty-four hours a day, so no I don't have a great deal of worry."

"You do have a little," Philip looked passed Leena, ignoring her existence.

"All that matters is that you can't hurt anyone anymore," Leena spoke, poised with authority.

"At the moment, no. Do you remember me saying that I have worked long and hard on building an army? I'll be saved, maybe not tonight, but I will always and forevermore be the King of Coleman. I'm not worried, but you should be. There are more things out there than you or your witchy friend can even dream of. It was so simple for me to take over the mind of the Kitsune! Believe me, I'm not staying here for long!"

"Then please explain why you are doing this?" Leena felt herself practically begging for Philip's cooperation.

"Because it's fun. It's entertaining to me that you don't care if you have lost a friend or not. Anything to prevent them from finding out the truth. Right?" Philip's smile grew more and more menacing with each passing second.

"What do you get out of this? What do you get out of me telling them that we are twins, that our parents chose separate birthdays just to spare our feelings, that we are connected in such a way that if one dies, the other is killed?" Leena barked, growing irritable. "No one wins, I lose if they find out that I am actually closer than they think to the serial killer of Coleman!"

"Twins?" a group of sorrow filled, and scared voices filled the room.

Smiling from ear to ear, Philip began to fill the room once again with laughter. Quickly spinning on her heels, Leena found herself face to face with not only Samuel, but Raphael, Mark, Matt, and James. Growing increasingly pale, more so than usual, Leena made a feeble attempt to rush to her friends. Tripping over her own feet, she fell hard on the floor, the sound of her body hitting the cement echoed through the precinct.

"Guys, no!" she screamed as the group turned from her, leaving the room. "How long were they there?" she turned to Philip; her voice trembled with hate.

"Oh, I'd say about the moment you began to go on your rant."

Rushing from the room of cells, Leena spun in circles, looking for any sign of her friends. Knowing the truth was spilled, she felt that this was just the beginning, there was no reason for him to hold back any longer. Running from the building, Leena hollered for the group, but they were gone, their trust in her was definitely gone. Standing outside of the building, Leena watched as the moon and stars filled the sky, darkness consumed the streets, and the Coleman night life began to flood the streets. The cold brushed against her skin, each inhale left her nose to feel frozen shut, she placed her hands over her mouth, exhaling to keep warm. Few people filled the sidewalks as they began to finish their late-night holiday shopping. Walking to the nearest bench, Leena chose it was best for her to stay away for the night. It wasn't the first time a cold bench doubled as a bed. Balling up, she closed her eyes, hid in her jacket and with no choice, waited for the morning sounds to wake her.

25

Days had passed, Leena bounced from bench to bench, even taking shelter in the occasional, large storm drain. No word from her friends or even a simple phone call from the captain. Checking her phone, which she kept powered by grabbing coffee at the café and sitting near the outlet, she noticed today was the wedding of Matt and James. Walking by a few buildings, she checked herself out in the windows. Disgusted with the way she looked, Leena rushed into the closest store, searching for something that looked remotely decent. There has to be things in the place that look nice and aren't a dress! She thought as she wandered the store. Rummaging through a few sale racks, she heard a familiar voice flow through her ears.

"Mark, I don't think James or Matt will complain if I were something "witchy," as you say," the young woman threw her hands up, forming air quotations.

"Bella, one day without looking stereotypical won't kill you."

"No, Mark! I am wearing this, they won't care, they think my style is cute," she smiled, her pearly white teeth and adorable acts forced Mark to smile in return.

Keeping herself hidden from her friends, she listened from behind a rack of clothing. Getting the occasional glare from random customers, she chose to ignore them as gaining information felt more important. Inching closer, she ducked into a circular rack of clothes, pulled a few jeans to the side to better hear the conversation.

"Don't you think it is time to call Leena?" Bella spoke softly.

"No, no I don't! She lied to us all, she kept major secrets for a month. I'm not going through this with you again, baby. According to Samuel, James and Matt are hesitant on even wanting her at the wedding. She knew everything Philip was going to do or did do, from kidnapping and killing your mother, in secret mind you, he wasn't even going to allow Luna's case to be closed. If it weren't for you, no one would have found her body. She kept blackmail letters a secret, among various other secrets. Knowing her, she will probably be a ghost for a while," Mark kept his voice down in the presence of mortals.

Emotions consumed Leena, her eyes welled with tears, her face felt warm with sorrow. Releasing the clothing, she fell back into the rack of half priced jeans. Rubbing her hands across her face, Leena wiped tear after tear away from her eyes. Anger, sadness, and regret filled her head. I don't even know where to begin with my apologies! She thought to herself, using a pair of jeans to wipe water from her cheeks. Looking out from the clothing rack, she saw no signs of her friends. Slowly climbing from under the jeans, she grabbed a few decent items of clothing, which included a light blue button up blouse and black slacks. Even if she was hated and feeling lost, she was going to look great for her friends. Even if she had to hide behind a tree to watch, she wanted to see the blessed event. Hating the bright colors didn't prevent her from caring for James and Matt. A fey wedding was always bright, magical, and filled with love and nature.

Exiting the store, she was brought to a stop as she collided with yet another familiar face. Falling to the sleety pavement, she looked up, meeting Raphael's gaze. Exhaustion filled him, bags under his eyes and untamed hair sat on his head. Sitting for a moment of silence, their mouths cracked a smile, happy to see at least one person that didn't hate them.

"Leena!"

"Raphe, hey, how have you been?" her voice soft, the past days taking a toll on her, leaving her an empty shell. That's how she felt at least.

"Good, I guess. I have no place to live, I've been living off of gas station sandwiches and Dr. Plasma. Neither of which is great, that I can say for sure."

"Eternal Night?" she questioned.

"Your brother did what he said he was going to do. He took it, I can't get near the place without being attacked!" Raphael's voice broke with each word. Losing the bar really took a toll on him, more than Leena actually knew.

"He's locked up! How the hell can he still control the place?"

"Must have some loyal ass followers. I tried to get my place back yesterday and was attacked by a pack of vampire hungry wolves! I'm no match for what resides within those walls. I may not have magical powers, but I can feel the crazy flowing from the walls."

The cold wind continued to beat at them, forcing them to find warmth. Walking hastily to the café, they looked around for an empty table. Quickly stealing the furthest table, they placed an order for warm Dr. Plasma, set their bags to the side and allowed a deep exhale to escape their lungs.

"So, are you still going to the wedding?" Leena spoke between drinks. Gulping down her Dr. Plasma like it was the last one she would ever get.

"Yeah, they messaged me earlier. They told me I could get ready at their place if need be. You?"

"Thinking I will watch from a distance. I know it is inside, but I may just peek through the window. Creepy I know, but I saw Mark and Bella while I was at the clothing store and it didn't really feel like I was welcome around the grooms," Leena's voice was cracking yet again.

"You remember it is this afternoon, right?" he looked to Leena, placing a hand on hers, hoping he could give some comfort.

Raphael may be one badass vampire, but he was good at pushing the hunger down and showing some true feelings. Smiling, Leena sat for a moment, speechless, she tossed a hand in the air signaling for another flask of synthetic blood. Pulling her hand away as her drink arrived, she kept looking at her phone, seemingly distracted by something unseen.

"Got a date?" he laughed.

"No Raphe, just scared."

"You? Scared?" Raphael spoke, his right brow slowly began to lift.

"Captain Sommers comes back from vacation today, it's the day of the wedding and all I can think of is what Philip was repeating," Leena looked from her phone, to Raphael, to the windows, acting very vigilant.

"I don't think he is going to kill the captain, let alone crash the wedding. He is locked up behind bars."

"It's his army that worries me. If they can prevent you from entering Eternal Night, I can only imagine what else they can do!" worry consumed each word that fell from her lips.

Spending the next couple of hours at the café, doing their best to stay out of the cold, they found themselves ordering food. To the humans, they probably looked like two hobo's, covered in dirt and dust. As the sun was breaking through the clouds, they knew it was time to begin preparing themselves for the wedding. Walking to the gym, the wind was harsh, whipping her hair into knots, she found herself complaining silently. They compelled the front desk to allow them entrance to the showers.

Going their separate ways, Leena kicked open the door to the showers. Scaring some innocent ladies, she ignored their words of annoyance. Twisting the handle, Leena waited patiently as the steam filled the shower cubicle. Carefully stepping into the shower, she allowed the almost boiling water to wash over her, like a wave of positivity. Using the soaps from the gym, she ran her hands through her hair, filling her sinuses with the smell of cucumber and rose. Suds ran down her pale, luscious body. Dirt and dust filled the base at her feet. Leaning against the wall, she closed her eyes and thought of Raphael just on the other side of the wall. Feeling a hand on her hip, she was brought back to reality, pulling the hand away.

"The hell are you doing?" she looked Raphael in the eyes, realizing he was naked, she pulled him into the shower. "This is the ladies locker room, dumbass!"

"Don't worry, compelled everyone to leave and I locked the door."

Ignoring his acts of idiocy, she pulled him close, the feeling of his chest and abs against her skin forced her to quiver. Leena knew they needed to hurry, but in this moment, she felt like Raphael was the only person who didn't hate her, she needed the release. Pushing her against the wall, water flowed over them as Leena grabbed ahold of his firm ass. Sensually pressing his lips to hers, they filled the room with moans and sighs of ecstasy. Running her hands over his muscles, she felt him tense up beneath her hands, forcing her to dig her claws into his skin. Quick to heel, he lifted her hands above her head, turned her to face the wall and kissed her neck, sending vibrations and shivers down her spine. With their acts of lust filling the shower room, they felt the water growing cold. Turning the shower off, they stood in each other's embrace, inhaling, and exhaling deeply, their naked bodies tangled in deep romance. Exiting the shower, Leena slapped Raphael's ass, watching as the muscle rippled, forcing him to spin quickly, a brow raised with a corner mouthed smile growing on his face.

Throwing on their clothing, they left the gym, once again entering the cold winds of November. Bracing themselves against the wind, they hailed a passing cab.

Sitting in silence, Raphael wrapped an arm around Leena, keeping her close. He knew she may not be the relationship type, hell he wasn't, but in that moment of closeness he didn't really care. Tapping the cabbie on the shoulder, they indicated that they would like him to pull over a block away from the building, hoping they wouldn't be seen. Jumping from the cab, Leena waited as Raphael gave the driver a few bucks.

26

"Guess this is where we part ways," Leena placed a hand to his cheek, lightly pulling him close, placing a tender kiss to his lips.

"I'll be right inside. I wish you'd try and come in," he spoke quietly. "If anything happens out here, give a shout, I'll hear you, love."

Watching Raphael walk into the building, Leena carefully walked around to get a view of the wedding. Using her supernatural hearing, she listened as music began to fill the room. Watching James and Matt enter from behind closed doors, holding hands and large smiles on their faces, Leena couldn't help but feel slightly emotional. People stood as they walked between the sets of chairs, throwing lavender and wreathes made of various flowers at their feet signifying the sacred, loving, and new bond they were about to make. Seeing Raphael take a seat in the middle, she smiled, happy she had him by her side.

As James and Matt approached the altar, they were greeted by Mark and Bella. Handing them each a candle, the crowd watched as James and Matt lit one candle, using it to light the other. As the wicks burned, the smoke emanating from them began to shape itself into a large dove. The sounds of happy guests filled the room as they watched in awe. The dove, now fully complete, looked as if it burst into hundreds of smaller, colorful doves that swirled around the couple, settling themselves on the wooden studs that stretched across the ceiling. Smiles grew on everyone's face as Mark placed himself behind the couple, opened a book and began to read a few words.

Watching Mark, Leena couldn't help but feel tears fill her eyes. The feeling of being alone, unloved, and hating herself felt almost too much for her. Throwing her emotions to the side, she focused solely on James and Matt. Looking around the room as best she could, she took in the beauty of their wedding. Noticing something tucked up in the ceiling, she squinted her eyes, hoping that she would be able to see whatever the object was. Horror ripped at her insides as she recognized an eerie looking character sitting up in the ceiling, holding a rope connected to a dark, unwelcoming tarp.

"What the hell?" she moved to another window, keeping as quiet as she could. "Shit!"

To her dismay, Leena recognized the man to be Philip. Looking to the altar, she saw that the ceremony was going smoothly. How the hell did he get out? She thought quickly of ways to distract him. Coming up empty handed on ways to control her brother, she rushed around the building. Standing just before the door, she was hesitant to enter. Why she froze, she couldn't figure out, but she knew she needed to act quickly. Barreling through the doors, she looked to the ceiling, hoping to startle Philip enough that he'd lose balance and crash down to Earth.

"No!" Leena's voice filled the room.

"Leena, what the hell are you doing?" James spun to face his friend. "No what?"

Realizing that she had interrupted the "I do's" she pulled a knife from under her blouse, tossing it in Philip's direction. Angered, he pulled the cord, filling the room with black roses, that fell slowly to the floor. Understanding the signal, a few other unwelcomed guests that were blending into the crowd jumped from the benches. Running from the building, Leena wasn't quick enough to stop them all. Philip, who was now at the altar, brought a hand in the air showing the guests a small device. Before anyone took the chance to stop him, he pressed his thumb against the button. The room was soon filled with a click and seconds after, an explosion that blew the glass from the windows, sending friends and family flying in different directions. The doors were blown from their hinges and debris covered the floor. Smoke and dust filled Leena's lungs as she frantically searched for Philip. Tripping over the occasional dead body and knocked out relative, she did her best to make way for the front of the building. Waving her hands in front of her face, she looked for any sign of James. Eyeing his shirt, she jumped over a bench, landing near her friend.

"James! James!" a shout from deep within brought James back to reality.

"Where is Matt? Matt! Matt, please!" James begged, hoping he didn't lose the love of his life.

Feeling a hand brush against his, James looked under a pile of debris just to his side. Pulling Matt to safety, he looked him deep in the eyes, kissed him and used each other to stand up, relaying on their support for stability. Looking around, James, Matt and Leena saw flames consuming the walls, reducing the curtains and flowers to ash and people panicking, in search of loved ones. Heavy smoke was flowing from the building, filling the air outside. Ash covered everyone's hair, dust covered their faces and blood stained their clothing. Pulling her phone from her pocket, she called the precinct, fire department and EMT's.

Matt was rushing around the room, helping people to safety when sorrow struck his mind. Looking to the floor, he saw Bella, lifeless in the arms of Mark, who was doing everything he could to bring her back to him. Knowing he didn't need help, the sorrow continued to flow through him as he saw his mother, father, and James' mother all dead, laying near the wall. Being the closest to the blast, Matt knew they didn't have a chance of survival. Hurrying to his side, Matt used what strength he could to keep James away from his dead mother. Falling to his knees, James held her in his arms, tears streaming down his face. People became unrecognizable as water blurred his vision. Hearing the emergency vehicle approaching the building, Leena rushed out the doors where a bloodied captain followed close behind.

"Detective! What in the hell happened?" Captain Sommers screamed, using a sleeve to wipe away a stream of blood that ran down from a deep laceration on her forehead.

"I don't have time to explain," she barked. "There are wounded inside, multiple deaths," she spoke, turning to the EMT's, guiding them in the right directions.

Gripping her arm, she pulled Leena close. Looking into Captain Sommers eyes, she had difficulty creating a full proper and cohesive sentence. Lauren tightened her grip, forcing Leena to let out a light growl.

"Speak! Now!"

"No! I will soon, I need to find him! I need answers!" Leena ripped her arm away from the captain. Running into the smoke that danced far from the building, Leena disappeared from sight.

Hours were spent pulling bodies from the aftermath of Philip's attack. People cried and held each other for comfort as the emergency vehicles were loaded with injured and the dead. The firefighters doused the flames that felt unwilling to die down. James, Matt, Mark, Raphael, and Lauren stood outside, watching the angry fire consume the place that was meant to be filled with joy and love.

"Raphael, where is Samuel?" both James and Matt spoke in unison, pain filled their words.

Looking around, he was brought to an immediate stop as his eyes connected with a figured that hadn't been fully zipped into a body bag. "There!" Raphael let out a boisterous howl, pointing to the ground. Rushing to the body, they all looked, filled with sadness as they gazed upon the lifeless corpse of Samuel Blackhorn. Matt held James close as the others stood, silently mourning for their lost co-worker. The group remained at the scene as day slowly turned to night, question after question was thrust upon them as newbie officers, detectives and help from Claresville did their best to write up reports. Pulling from the group, Matt and James after a while found some time to be alone.

"How are you, my love?" Matt looked James over for any sign of major injuries.

"Sad, pissed, in pain, all of the above! I'm sorry I couldn't give you the day you deserved!" James' eyes filled with tears.

"It was beautiful while it lasted, James. We will focus on family and friends, after that we will go to the court and get this finalized. I love you, more than you'll ever imagine!" Matt kissed James softly on the lips, hoping to not cause him anymore pain.

"I love you to Pluto and back," James smiled, holding Matt's hand gently.

With night finally taking over the day, they were all escorted to the hospital for further tests and medical treatments. As the group was rushed to the hospital, the sounds of sirens filled their ears as the vehicles sped off to the emergency room. Dodging car after car, the ambulance team weaved in and out of traffic, skipping the occasional red light. Upon arrival at the emergency room, Raphael, Mark, and Captain Sommers were all rushed to different rooms, where James and Matt were kept together. The jaws of life couldn't even pull them apart in that moment, they were by each other's side, no matter what. A growl would escape Matt's mouth each time a doctor tried to separate them. Listening to the doors close behind them, they leaned back in their beds, closed their eyes as the exhaustion soon took over.

27

A week had passed since the destroyed wedding and Philip's attack. The team was cleared for work and those who lost family and friends had already begun the process of taking care of funeral arrangements. Leena was nowhere to be found, she ignored phone calls and messages left by her friends and even Captain Sommers. Unaware that she lost Samuel, she avoided work and daylight at all costs. The morning was cold, dreary, some would say that the Earth was mourning the losses.

Arriving at the Coleman Police Department, Leena made her way to the guarded front doors. Flashing her badge, the two guards stepped aside, giving her a look of death and disgust. Sliding her keycard through the reader, one of the patrolmen pressed a few buttons giving her access to the building. A few steps into the room, Leena was met by a short, plump man.

"Gun, badge and anything metal, please place in a bin," a raspy voice echoed through the room, the man must have smoked most of his life.

Sliding the bin through the x-ray machine, Leena slowly walked under the body scanner. Without a beep hindering her from continuing, she stood, awaiting the arrival of her belongings. As the machine spat out the bin, she grabbed her badge, placed her gun back in its holster and made way for the elevators. Pressing the green button, Leena waited patiently for the silver doors to slid open. A loud ding erupted from the speaker, indicating the elevator had arrived at her floor.

The metallic doors slowly slid open, revealing a well-dressed, rather proper woman. Seemingly irritated, more to the point, she seemed pissed off, the woman stepped to the side allowing Leena entrance into the small room. As the doors closed, Leena looked over, hesitant to speak.

"Captain Sommers," Leena spoke, giving a slight nod. "Tough morning?" she did everything she could to brush off the fact that if Lauren Sommers had the means to do so, she would've ripped Leena limb from limb

"I want you in my office, promptly! By promptly I mean the moment you exit this goddamned elevator, your ass better be seated across from me!" the woman barked. Leena knew better than to question.

"Yes sir."

The rest of the elevator ride was left silent. Another ding announced the arrival of the elevator to the office floor. Once more, the doors slowly slid open, revealing yet another familiar face. James stood, arm crossed and clearly pissed. This was not going to be a good day for Leena.

"What's wrong?" Leena spoke, stepping from the elevator. "You seem irritated."

"Do I?" anger, frustration and exhaustion filled the space.

"Okay! What the hell did I do?"

"Nothing! That's exactly the problem. You couldn't even make it to the wedding, which your brother crashed and killed a lot of people by the way! Including both of our parents, Matt is taking it really hard! You were gone for a week and you made no attempt to apologize for anything, lies or otherwise!"

"Okay, that's not my fault! Besides, he had been locked up! I had no idea he escaped, or who even helped him"

"All the more reason for you to be focused, and you know, maybe show up to work!" he turned to walk away. "Your brother, he left you a letter!"

Leaving Leena to stand alone, she knew it was going to take a great deal of time and effort for James to forgive her. Strutting towards Captain Sommers office, Leena would get the occasional glance from a co-worker. Standing between the office and the hallway, Leena lightly rapped on the door.

"Sit!" Captain Sommers pointed at the empty chair. Avoiding eye contact with Leena.

"Can I just start with how sorry?"

"No, no you can't!" she interrupted.

"Look, sir, I don't know how he escaped."

"He left you a letter," she bellowed, throwing the letter at Leena, striking her in the face, the envelope gave her a slight cut. "What pisses me off the most is that you had no desire to inform me, me the fucking captain, your boss, that your brother was the one murdering people! Raphael helped me to realize the only reason I took vacation was because Philip managed to compel me to leave! Is there any reason why you decided to leave this information out?"

"I didn't feel it necessary, I thought I could take care of him," Leena turned the envelope over in her hands, unwilling to let any other words leave her lips. Her voice was soft, cautious.

"Well, I wonder if me putting you on a very long non-paid, leave of absence would allow you to feel future news like that to be necessary!" she barked. "You may leave my office, now! Don't forget your damn letter and report to my office on Monday!" she waved Leena out the door.

"Yes sir," Leena mouthed quietly.

Making her way to her desk, she ignored a glance from James. Witnessing the mess that she called a desk, Leena tossed the letter on her keyboard, threw some papers to the side, and crashed into her chair. Grabbing the small knife, she sliced through the envelope, struck with pain as the opener caught her finger. Sucking the blood from her wound, she gently opened the letter, mouthing the words, silently.

"Son of a bitch," she whispered to herself. Dropping her hand to her side, she left a small, bloody thumbprint on the corner of the letter. Looking out the window, dark, eerie clouds grew close, and snow fell from the sky making visibility impossible.

28

December came and went in the blink of an eye. Leena spent the month alone, her friends ignoring her every phone call. The holidays were, in Leena's eyes cold and lifeless. With no place to stay, Leena found herself bouncing from bench to bench. She would add the occasional hotel room to her list or even sleeping at the Coffee House Café, that is after spending hours begging the owner. The month was cold, filled with blizzards and even a horrendous, unforgiving ice storm. Which according to the meteorologist was the worst they've had since the late 70's.

Leena knew that the New Year was beginning to inch its way closer and with that, it meant bountiful new and interesting murders. She found herself having to spend the next full moon alone, vulnerable. Blacking out from the pain of the change, she doesn't even remember who she killed—if she killed. Leena spent almost all of December wandering the streets alone, of course that was after a long day at work, being ignored by friends and co-workers. Hell, Captain Sommers forced her to work without pay. Illegal of course, but who is she to care? Any downtime that Leena was awarded she would spend calling Mark, James and even Raphael. With the death of Samuel looming over her, Leena knew that her life would never feel the same. Filled with lies and loss, sorrow and defeat, she felt the struggle of going day to day. Even starving herself, attempting to take her own life didn't work as the hybrid in her kept her alive. Feeling like she had lost everything, Leena would never give up on getting her friends back.

Swiping across Mark's name on her new phone, she patiently waited for him to answer. She knew he wouldn't, but she didn't want to give up. "Mark? Hey man it's me, again. It's the 30th, almost the New Year. I was wondering if we were still on to party?" Leena spoke, her voice horse, filled with sadness.

Leaving voicemail after voicemail, she made an abundance of phones calls. At least 20 feeble attempts to speak with her friends. As the morning grew colder, she knew people would begin to flood the café. Gathering what little belongings she had, Leena threw on a quick change of clothing, stole a cup of coffee, tossed on her ripped jacket, and made her way outside. The violent winds whipped around her, causing Leena to tuck her face into the warmth of her jacket. Wishing it weren't as torn as it was, she looked for her next stop, any place that would keep her warm. Eyeing the entrance to Relic Book and Candle, Leena set her gaze upon the building, hoping that the new owner, Luna's sister, would grant her access. Dodging snow that fell from the roofs and avoiding slush flung by speeding cars, she unknowingly collided with a hooded figure.

"You should probably watch where the hell you're going!" a familiar voice to Leena pierced her ears.

"Sorry. Wait, Matt?"

"Oh, Leena, hi," he gave a small smile, careful not to show her too much compassion.

"How are you?" Leena asked softly, exhaustion filled her words and her actions.

"Uh, I am doing well. I should really be going."

Nodding her head, showing she understood, she began to walk away. Looking back to her friend, she quickly found herself loosing balance as she took a step, finding hidden black ice. Connecting hard with the pavement beneath her, Leena tried to break her fall by placing her arm near her head. A failed attempt as the side of her head bashed against the sidewalk, cracking open her skull and chipping the frozen concrete.

"Leena!" Matt yelped. "Are you okay?" he added, kneeling by her side, helping her slowly sit up.

"I'm fine, just go. I'm sure James is waiting for you."

"Come with me. Please?" Matt placed a hand on her back and one on her arm.

Slowly bringing Leena to her feet, he was careful to keep his hands steady, guiding her to safe ground. Making their way to the Hometown Pizzeria, Matt gave Leena the update on the past few weeks. Protecting her as best he could, he noticed that every so often Leena would look to him with a smile, being careful to not allow him to see her soft side.

"Well it has been awfully busy at the precinct, as you know. James and I had a beautiful honeymoon, in Florida, of course this was after all the funerals. We spent some time on the beach and did a great deal of shopping. Which reminds me, we brought you back a little something," Matt spoke, brushing off the snow that began to collect on his stubble.

"And Mark?"

"Oh, well we haven't really seen much of him. After you disappeared, he kind of spiraled out of control, couldn't really deal with the loss of Bella."

"That and I guess after finding out that Austin was still alive, and Philip was the cause of everything, being death and deceit, I could see him losing a bit of control."

"You know none of us are really happy with your brother, right? I mean he compelled Austin, Megan, Samuel and even Raphael to do unspeakable things."

"Don't remind me, Please?" Leena spoke, her voice choked, tears welled in her eyes, the cold wind burning her cracked skull which took its sweet time to heal.

Approaching the pizzeria, Leena eyed James who was flagging down his husband. Bringing his gesture to an abrupt stop, he gave Leena the glare of death. Understanding that James was in no condition to place forgiveness, Leena lowered her gaze slightly, continuing in his direction with Matt's caring guidance. Gently sitting herself at the table, Matt left her side placing a gentle, loving kiss on James' forehead. He whispered in Matt's ear, unwilling to allow Leena the opportunity to make out his words. Ignoring her friends semi childish acts, Leena dabbed a napkin against her head, cleaning up some of the dried blood.

"James? Can I please say something without you throwing a knife at my head?" she asked, pain filled her words as she continued to dab at her wound.

A deep sigh escaped his mouth. "Sure," he added, hiding his anger with irritation.

"I know what I did weeks ago was wrong, but can I please have a chance to explain?"

"No!" James kept his voice as low as possible. "I'm really not ready to listen. You were, are one of my best friends, but you missed the wedding, intentionally or not, you still didn't show. You lied to us all in different ways and then vanished," he fixed himself in the chair, grabbing his drink, allowing Leena to sit and stew.

Biting her lower lip, Leena's eyes began to well with tears once again. Rubbing her eyes, she tried hard as hell to hide her emotions. Using the dust in my eyes excuse, she excused herself from the table. Looking around the area, she saw a young woman leave the restroom, knowing this was her chance, she made a quick getaway, hoping James and Matt didn't see her shedding a tear. Kicking open the door, she checked the room, hoping to be alone. Silence filled the air as Leena looked in the mirror, her wound still trickled blood.

"Quit being such a sappy, whiny bitch," she spoke to herself in the mirror, cleaning herself up as best she could. "You made some mistakes, you're not the only one who has!" she did everything she could to boost her feelings.

"Little lady, may I speak?" a soft, loving, and shaky voice filled the room.

Leena looked around the bathroom, kicked open the stalls, looking for whoever was eavesdropping. Facing the mirrors, she saw a small mist beginning to form just behind her. Spinning on her heels, she found herself face to face with a manifesting, elderly woman.

"Who are you?" Leena raised a brow; curiosity began to fill her thoughts.

"Sandy, Sandy Millington."

"Okay, Sandy, care to explain why you were listening in on me?" Leena did her best not to be angry with the old spirit.

"When you've been here as long as I have dear, you find that listening in on sad and even happy people passes the time quickly."

"How long have you been here?" Leena spoke softly, being sure to not alert the workers and customers that she was talking to anyone. As it was a spirit, if one isn't supernatural, they wouldn't see the woman anyway.

"What year is it?"

"2018, December," Leena spoke, checking her phone just to be exact.

"Eighteen years my dear," Sandy spoke softly. "One day I came in with my husband for our weekly dinner, ordered our usual and the next thing I remember is watching my beloved Gary, crying over my body, holding me in his lap. I loved him; he was my everything. Gary was so kind and loving; he didn't have a mean bone in his body. I see him come in here every so often, order our usual and cry as he sips coffee, slowly eating the coffee cake that we would share," she added, hovering back and forth.

Leena couldn't hold back any more emotions, tears streamed down her face, her sobbing almost uncontrollable. Ripping a small paper towel from the machine, she rubbed the water from her eyes, her cracked skull began to throb. Turning back to the older woman, Leena attempted to place a hand on her shoulder. Her hand went through, no action from Sandy, only wide, forgetful eyes from Leena.

"Sorry. I thought I could, I'm sorry," Leena spoke, pools of water made visibility almost impossible.

The old woman raised a gentle hand, placing it on Leena's cheek. Brushing the tears away, she looked Leena deep in the eyes. Giving her a smile, she kissed her on the forehead, pulling her in for a hug.

How can she hug me, but I can't touch her? Leena thought to herself as the woman gently embraced her. Giving her the shaking grandmother hug that we all know and love.

"It all seems rough, but when you've seen life the way I have, you begin to understand that no matter how much hate someone has for you, love will always take over," she smiled, again giving Leena a kiss to the cheek.

What is with old people giving kisses? Why do they love to console us? More so me, I'm over a thousand years old! Leena smiled with the thought.

Pulling away from Sandy, she saw as the older woman began to fade into nothingness. Using another handful of paper towels, Leena wiped away tears and fixed her runny nose. Looking hard into the mirror, her gaze was broken by a loud thump against the door.

"You alright in there?" Matt's voice broke her concentration.

"Be just a minute!" she cleaned up the area, placed another towel to her head and made way for the door. Greeting her on the other side of the door was not only Matt, but James as well. Drinks in hand, they once again helped Leena get to the table. Sliding over a large flask of Dr. Plasma, James smiled. Sipping the drink, Leena kept an eye on both her friends, wondering how James could go from prissy to smiley in just a few minutes. Listening to James and Matt laugh and talk about their day, Leena couldn't help but feel out of place, like she was in an entirely different world. With the ringing of her phone breaking the conversation, Leena stepped aside to avoid upsetting her friends.

"Hello," she kept her voice quiet.

"Good morning, sister," the voice on the other end forced Leena to shiver. Drawing fear into her mind, she looked back to Matt and James, hoping they weren't trying to listen.

"What the fuck do you want? I'll kill you, you're first on my list!" Leena let a deep growl leave her throat, her words filled with anger. Using her fear and pain to fuel her hate. Her blood boiled, her fangs grew, and her hand clenched the phone almost crushing the device.

Laughing on the other end of the phone, Philip was showing no verbal signs of fear, not even a catch in his throat. Filling her ears with devilish chuckling, Leena found herself pulling the phone away for fear of the boisterous noise blowing out her eardrum. Walking further from the table, Leena tried to avoid the glares of innocent humans trying to enjoy breakfast.

"Look, you son of a bitch! I don't care how long it takes or where you are, I will hunt your ass down! And when I do, I will take great pleasure in ripping you apart, limb from limb!" Leena continued to try and keep her voice down.

"Good luck! Remember if I die, you die" he spoke without fear, leaving Leena to listen to the dial tone.

Leaning against the wall, she placed her head against a pillar. Forgetting that she had a wound, she jerked her head away, quickly placing a hand to the once again bleeding laceration. Shaking off the pain, she stumbled back to the table. Ignoring the looks from James, she chugged the rest of her Dr. Plasma. Ordering a few more rounds of the synthetic blood, she could feel herself healing, getting stronger with each sip. The morning was beginning to grow into the afternoon, the sun tried to peek between the clouds.

"So, what are your plans for the day? For the weekend?" Leena polished off her last drink. Yet again filling her friend's ears with lies.

Matt looked to James, hesitant to answer. Receiving a nod of approval, Matt spoke softly. "Going to Mark's place for a New Year's party tomorrow. Today, just doing some shopping, enjoying some time together."

"Oh?" Leena's word was filled with sadness. She couldn't even try to hide her emotions; James saw right through it.

"I'm sure you could tag along. I don't think he would really mind. May be a fun surprise for him," James smiled to Leena, the smile that could melt any heart.

"He hasn't even answered any of my calls, I don't think I should show up unannounced on his doorstep," Leena slouched in her chair, brushing the hair from her face, wiping away the dried blood that was left over from her fall.

"Just come with us, and for tonight you can stay at our place. No reason for you to stay out in the cold," Matt interjected, looking to James for backup.

Packing up their belongings, they placed some cash out on the table, pushed open the door and began the search for their vehicle. The sun was trying to melt some of the snow left over from the storm the night before. Falling into the car, they turned up the heat, listened to the radio, pulled out into the Coleman traffic, and made off to continue the holiday weekend. Hesitant as she was, Leena was hoping for some sort of redemption at Mark's New Year's party. Placing her head against the headrest, she closed her eyes, ignored the music, and fell into a deep nap, the warmth of the car hugged her like a freshly dried blanket.

ABOUT THE AUTHOR

BRANDON M. THAMKE is an American YA, Fantasy, Erotica, Romance, Horror and Science Fiction writer. He is best known for the retired Leena Rose, Vampire Detective Series, a 2020 Barnes & Noble bestseller. It has since been retired and the characters given a new path as seen in THE DARKEST ROSE and soon to be FROZEN ROSE. He likes to spend his downtime enjoying his many hobbies and traveling to as many places as he can. He and his husband live in a small town in Iowa. He has always been a fan of the supernatural, undead, and mythological folklore, which led him to follow his career as an author.

Made in the USA

www.ingramcontent.com/pod-product-compliance
Lightning Source LLC
LaVergne TN
LVHW050959080826
845145LV00009B/2355

* 9 7 8 1 7 3 6 9 5 6 5 6 4 *